Under The Red Robe

1896

STANLEY JOHN WEYMAN

TABLE OF CONTENTS

AT ZATON'S

"Marked cards!"

There were a score round us when the fool, little knowing the man with whom he had to deal, and as little how to lose like a gentleman, flung the words in my teeth. He thought, I'll be sworn, that I should storm and swear and ruffle it like any common cock of the hackle. But that was never Gil de Berault's way. For a few seconds after he had spoken I did not even look at him. I passed my eye instead--smiling, bien entendu--round the ring of waiting faces, saw that there was no one except De Pombal I had cause to fear; and then at last I rose and looked at the fool with the grim face I have known impose on older and wiser men.

"Marked cards, M. l'Anglais?" I said, with a chilling sneer. "They are used, I am told, to trap players--not unbirched schoolboys."

"Yet I say that they are marked!" he replied hotly, in his queer foreign jargon. "In my last hand I had nothing. You doubled the stakes. Bah, Sir, you knew! You have swindled me!"

"Monsieur is easy to swindle--when he plays with a mirror behind him," I answered tartly. And at that there was a great roar of laughter, which might have been heard in the street, and which brought to the table every one in the eating-house whom his violence had not already attracted. But I did not relax my face. I waited until all was quiet again, and then waving aside two or three who stood between us and the entrance, I pointed gravely to the door. "There is a little space behind the church of St. Jacques, M. l'Etranger," I said, putting on my hat and taking my cloak on my arm. "Doubtless you will accompany me thither?"

He snatched up his hat, his face burning with shame and rage. "With pleasure!" he blurted out. "To the devil, if you like!"

I thought the matter arranged, when the Marquis laid his hand on the young fellow's arm and checked him. "This must not be," he said, turning from him to me with his grand fine-gentleman's air. "You know me, M. de Berault. This matter has gone far enough."

"Too far, M. de Pombal!" I answered bitterly. "Still, if you wish to take the gentleman's place, I shall raise no objection."

"Chut, man!" he retorted, shrugging his shoulders negligently. "I know you, and I do not fight with men of your stamp. Nor need this gentleman."

"Undoubtedly," I replied, bowing low, "if he prefers to be caned in the streets."

That stung the Marquis. "Have a care! have a care!" he cried hotly. "You go too far, M. Berault."

"De Berault, if you please," I objected, eyeing him sternly. "My family has borne the de as long as yours, M. de Pombal."

He could not deny that, and he answered, "As you please"; at the same time restraining his friend by a gesture. "But none the less, take my advice," he continued. "The Cardinal has forbidden duelling, and this time he means it! You have been in trouble once and gone free. A second time it may fare worse with you. Let this gentleman go, therefore, M. de Berault. Besides-- why, shame upon you, man!" he exclaimed hotly; "he is but a lad!"

Two or three who stood behind me applauded that. But I turned and they met my eye; and they were as mum as mice. "His age is his own concern," I said grimly. "He was old enough a while ago to insult me."

"And I will prove my words!" the lad cried, exploding at last. He had spirit enough, and the Marquis had had hard work to restrain him so long. "You do me no service, M. de Pombal," he continued, pettishly shaking off his friend's hand. "By your leave, this gentleman and I will settle this matter."

"That is better," I said, nodding drily, while the Marquis stood aside, frowning and baffled. "Permit me to lead the way."

Zaton's eating-house stands scarcely a hundred paces from St. Jacques la Boucherie, and half the company went thither with us. The evening was wet, the light in the streets was waning, the streets themselves were dirty and slippery. There were few passers in the Rue St. Antoine; and our party, which earlier in the day must have attracted notice and a crowd, crossed unmarked, and entered without interruption the paved triangle which lies immediately behind the church. I saw in the distance one of the Cardinal's guard loitering in front of the scaffolding round the new Hôtel Richelieu; and the sight of the uniform gave me pause for a moment. But it was too late to repent.

The Englishman began at once to strip off his clothes. I closed mine to the throat, for the air was chilly. At that moment, while we stood preparing and most of the company seemed a little inclined to stand off from me, I felt a hand on my arm, and, turning, saw the dwarfish tailor at whose house in the Rue Savonnerie I lodged at the time. The fellow's presence was unwelcome, to say the least of it; and though for want of better company I had sometimes encouraged him to be free with me at home, I took that to be no reason why I should be plagued with him before gentlemen. I shook him off, therefore, hoping by a frown to silence him.

He was not to be so easily put down, however. And perforce I had to speak to him. "Afterwards, afterwards," I said. "I am engaged now."

"For God's sake, don't, Sir!" was the poor fool's answer. "Don't do it! You will bring a curse on the house. He is but a lad, and--"

"You, too!" I exclaimed, losing patience. "Be silent, you scum! What do you know about gentlemen's quarrels? Leave me; do you hear?"

"But the Cardinal!" he cried in a quavering voice. "The Cardinal, M. de Berault? The last man you killed is not forgotten yet. This time he will be sure to--"

"Do you hear?" I hissed. The fellow's impudence passed all bounds. It was as bad as his croaking. "Begone!" I said. "I suppose you are afraid he will kill me, and you will lose your money?"

Frison fell back at that almost as if I had struck him, and I turned to my adversary, who had been awaiting my motions with impatience. God knows he did look young; as he stood with his head bare and his fair hair drooping over his smooth woman's forehead--a mere lad fresh from the College of Burgundy, if they have such a thing in England. I felt a sudden chill as I looked at him: a qualm, a tremor, a presentiment. What was it the little tailor had said? That I should--but there, he did not know. What did he know of such things? If I let this pass I must kill a man a day, or leave Paris and the eating-house, and starve.

"A thousand pardons," I said gravely, as I drew and took my place. "A dun. I am sorry that the poor devil caught me so inopportunely. Now, however, I am at your service."

He saluted, and we crossed swords and began. But from the first I had no doubt what the result would be. The slippery stones and fading light gave him, it is true, some chance, some advantage, more than he deserved; but I had no sooner felt his blade than I knew that he was no swordsman. Possibly he had taken half-a-dozen lessons in rapier art, and practised what he learned with an Englishman as heavy and awkward as himself. But that was all. He made a few wild, clumsy rushes, parrying widely. When I had foiled these, the danger was over, and I held him at my mercy.

I played with him a little while, watching the sweat gather on his brow, and the shadow of the church-tower fall deeper and darker, like the shadow of doom, on his face. Not out of cruelty--God knows I have never erred in that direction!--but because, for the first time in my life, I felt a strange reluctance to strike the blow. The curls clung to his forehead; his breath came and went in gasps; I heard the men behind me murmur, and one or two of them drop an oath; and then I slipped--slipped, and was down in a moment on my right side, my elbow striking the pavement so sharply that the arm grew numb to the wrist.

He held off! I heard a dozen voices cry, "Now! now you have him!" But he held off. He stood back and waited with his breast heaving and his point lowered, until I had risen and stood again on my guard.

"Enough! enough!" a rough voice behind me cried. "Don't hurt the man after that."

"On guard, Sir!" I answered coldly--for he seemed to waver. "It was an accident. It shall not avail you again."

Several voices cried "Shame!" and one, "You coward!" But the Englishman stepped forward, a fixed look in his blue eyes. He took his place without a word. I read in his drawn white face that he had made up his mind to the worst, and his courage won my admiration. I would gladly and thankfully have set one of the lookers-on--any of the lookers-on--in his place; but that could not be. So I thought of Zaton's closed to me, of Pombal's insult, of the sneers and slights I had long kept at the sword's point; and, pressing him suddenly in a heat of affected anger, I thrust strongly over his guard, which had grown feeble, and ran him through the chest.

When I saw him lying, laid out on the stones with his eyes half shut, and his face glimmering white in the dusk--not that I saw him thus long, for there were a dozen kneeling round him in a twinkling--I felt an unwonted pang. It passed, however, in a moment. For I found myself confronted by a ring of angry faces--of men who, keeping at a distance, hissed and threatened me.

They were mostly canaille, who had gathered during the fight, and had viewed all that passed from the farther side of the railings. While some snarled and raged at me like wolves, calling me "Butcher!" and "Cut-throat!" and the like, or cried out that Berault was at his trade again, others threatened me with the vengeance of the Cardinal, flung the edict in my teeth, and said with glee that the guard were coming--they would see me hanged yet.

"His blood is on your head!" one cried furiously. "He will be dead in an hour. And you will swing for him! Hurrah!"

"Begone to your kennel!" I answered, with a look which sent him a yard backwards, though the railings were between us. And I wiped my blade carefully, standing a little apart. For--well, I could understand it--it was one of those moments when a man is not popular. Those who had come with me from the eating-house eyed me askance, and turned their backs when I drew nearer; and those who had joined us and obtained admission were scarcely more polite.

But I was not to be outdone in sangfroid. I cocked my hat, and drawing my cloak over my shoulders, went out with a swagger which drove the curs from the gate before I came within a dozen paces of it. The rascals outside fell back as quickly, and in a moment I was in the street. Another moment and I should have been clear of the place and free to lie by for a while, when a sudden scurry took place round me. The crowd fled every way into the gloom, and in a hand-turn a dozen of the Cardinal's guard closed round me.

I had some acquaintance with the officer in command, and he saluted me civilly. "This is a bad business, M. de Berault," he said. "The man is dead they tell me."

"Neither dying nor dead," I answered lightly. "If that be all, you may go home again."

"With you," he replied, with a grin, "certainly. And as it rains, the sooner the better. I must ask you for your sword, I am afraid."

"Take it," I said, with the philosophy which never deserts me. "But the man will not die."

"I hope that may avail you," he answered in a tone I did not like. "Left wheel, my friends! To the Châtelet! March!"

"There are worse places," I said, and resigned myself to fate. After all, I had been in prison before, and learned that only one jail lets no prisoner escape.

But when I found that my friend's orders were to hand me over to the watch, and that I was to be confined like any common jail-bird caught cutting a purse or slitting a throat, I confess my heart sank. If I could get speech with the Cardinal, all would probably be well; but if I failed in this, or if the case came before him in strange guise, or he were in a hard mood himself, then it might go ill with me. The edict said, death!

And the lieutenant at the Châtelet did not put himself to much trouble to hearten me. "What! again, M. de Berault?" he said, raising his eyebrows as he received me at the gate, and recognized me by the light of the brazier which his men were just kindling outside. "You are a very bold man, Sir, or a very foolhardy one, to come here again. The old business, I suppose?"

"Yes, but he is not dead," I answered coolly.

"He has a trifle--a mere scratch. It was behind the church of St. Jacques."

"He looked dead enough," my friend the guardsman interposed. He had not yet gone.

"Bah!" I answered scornfully. "Have you ever known me make a mistake? When I kill a man, I kill him. I put myself to pains, I tell you, not to kill this Englishman. Therefore he will live."

"I hope so," the lieutenant said, with a dry smile. "And you had better hope so, too, M. de Berault. For if not--"

"Well?" I said, somewhat troubled. "If not, what, my friend?"

"I fear he will be the last man you will fight," he answered. "And even if he lives, I would not be too sure, my friend. This time the Cardinal is determined to put it down."

"He and I are old friends," I said confidently.

"So I have heard," he answered, with a short laugh. "I think the same was said of Chalais. I do not remember that it saved his head."

This was not reassuring. But worse was to come. Early in the morning orders were received that I should be treated with especial strictness, and I was given the choice between irons and one of the cells below the level. Choosing the latter, I was left to reflect upon many things; among others, on the queer and uncertain nature of the Cardinal, who loved, I knew, to play with a man as a cat with a mouse; and on the ill effects which sometimes attend a high chest-thrust, however carefully delivered. I only rescued myself at last from these and other unpleasant reflections by obtaining the loan of a pair of dice; and the light being just enough to enable me to reckon the throws, I amused myself for hours by casting them on certain principles of my own. But a long run again and again upset my calculations; and at last brought me to the conclusion that a run of bad luck may be so persistent as to see out the most sagacious player. This was not a reflection very welcome to me at the moment.

Nevertheless, for three days it was all the company I had. At the end of that time the knave of a jailer who attended me, and who had never grown tired of telling me, after the fashion of his kind, that I should be hanged, came to me with a less assured air. "Perhaps you would like a little water?" he said civilly.

"Why, rascal?" I asked.

"To wash with," he answered.

"I asked for some yesterday, and you would not bring it," I grumbled. "However, better late than never. Bring it now. If I must hang, I will hang like a gentleman. But, depend upon it, the Cardinal will not serve an old friend so scurvy a trick."

"You are to go to him," he answered, when he came back with the water.

"What? To the Cardinal?" I cried.

"Yes," he answered.

"Good!" I exclaimed; and in my joy I sprang up at once, and began to refresh my dress. "So all this time I have been doing him an injustice. Vive Monseigneur! I might have known it."

"Don't make too sure!" the man answered spitefully. Then he went on: "I have something else for you. A friend of yours left it at the gate," he added. And he handed me a packet.

"Quite so!" I said, reading his rascally face aright. "And you kept it as long as you dared--as long as you thought I should hang, you knave! Was not that so? But there, do not lie to me. Tell me instead which of my friends left it." For, to confess the truth, I had not so many friends at this time; and ten good crowns--the packet contained no less a sum--argued a pretty staunch friend, and one of whom a man might be proud.

The knave sniggered maliciously. "A crooked, dwarfish man left it," he said. "I doubt I might call him a tailor and not be far out."

"Chut!" I answered; but I was a little out of countenance. "I understand. An honest fellow enough, and in debt to me! I am glad he remembered. But when am I to go, friend?"

"In an hour," he answered sullenly. Doubtless he had looked to get one of the crowns; but I was too old a hand for that. If I came back I could buy his services; and if I did not I should have wasted my money.

Nevertheless, a little later, when I found myself on my way to the Hôtel Richelieu under so close a guard that I could see nothing except the figures that immediately surrounded me, I wished I had given him the money. At such times, when all hangs in the balance and the sky is overcast, the mind runs on luck and old superstitions, and is prone to think a crown given here may avail there--though there be a hundred leagues away.

The Palais Richelieu was at this time in building, and we were required to wait in a long, bare gallery, where the masons were at work. I was kept a full hour here, pondering uncomfortably on the strange whims and fancies of the great man who then ruled France as the King's Lieutenant-General, with all the King's powers; and whose life I had once been the means of saving by a little timely information. On occasion he had done something to wipe out the debt; and at other times he had permitted me to be free with him. We were not unknown to one another, therefore.

Nevertheless, when the doors were at last thrown open, and I was led into his presence, my confidence underwent a shock. His cold glance, that, roving over me, regarded me not as a man but an item, the steely glitter of his southern eyes, chilled me to the bone. The room was bare, the floor without carpet or covering. Some of the woodwork lay about, unfinished and in pieces. But the man--this man, needed no surroundings. His keen, pale face, his brilliant eyes, even his presence--though he was of no great height and began already to stoop at the shoulders--were enough to awe the boldest. I recalled as I looked at him a hundred tales of his iron will, his cold heart, his unerring craft. He had humbled the King's brother, the splendid Duke of Orleans, in the dust. He had curbed the Queen-mother. A dozen heads, the noblest in France, had come to the block through him. Only two years before he had quelled Rochelle; only a few months before he had crushed the great insurrection in Languedoc: and though the south, stripped of its old privileges, still seethed with discontent, no one in this year 1630 dared lift a hand against him--openly, at any rate. Under the surface a hundred plots, a thousand intrigues, sought his life or his power; but these, I suppose, are the hap of every great man.

No wonder, then, that the courage on which I plumed myself sank low at sight of him; or that it was as much as I could do to mingle with the humility of my salute some touch of the sangfroid of old acquaintanceship.

And perhaps that had been better left out. For this man was without bowels. For a moment, while he stood looking at me and before he spoke to me, I gave myself up for lost. There was a glint of cruel satisfaction in his eyes that warned me, before he spoke, what he was going to say to me.

"I could not have made a better catch, M. de Berault," he said, smiling villainously, while he gently smoothed the fur of a cat that had sprung on the table beside him. "An old offender and an excellent example. I doubt it will not stop with you. But later, we will make you the warrant for flying at higher game."

"Monseigneur has handled a sword himself," I blurted out. The very room seemed to be growing darker, the air colder. I was never nearer fear in my life.

"Yes?" he said, smiling delicately. "And so?"

"Will not be too hard on the failings of a poor gentleman."

"He shall suffer no more than a rich one," he replied suavely, as he stroked the cat. "Enjoy that satisfaction, M. de Berault. Is that all?"

"Once I was of service to your Eminence," I said desperately.

"Payment has been made," he answered, "more than once. But for that I should not have seen you, M. de Berault."

"The King's face!" I cried, snatching at the straw he seemed to hold out.

He laughed cynically, smoothly. His thin face, his dark moustache, and whitening hair, gave him an air of indescribable keenness. "I am not the King," he said. "Besides, I am told you have killed as many as six men in duels. You owe the King, therefore, one life at least. You must pay it. There is no more to be said, M. de Berault," he continued coldly, turning away and beginning to collect some papers. "The law must take its course."

I thought he was about to nod to the lieutenant to withdraw me, and a chilling sweat broke out down my back. I saw the scaffold, I felt the cords. A moment, and it would be too late! "I have a favour to ask," I stammered desperately, "if your Eminence would give me a moment alone."

"To what end?" he answered, turning and eyeing me with cold disfavour. "I know you--your past--all. It can do no good, my friend."

"Nor harm!" I cried. "And I am a dying man, Monseigneur!"

"That is true," he said thoughtfully. Still he seemed to hesitate; and my heart beat fast. At last he looked at the lieutenant. "You may leave us," he said shortly. "Now," when the officer had withdrawn and left us alone, "what is it? Say what you have to say quickly. And above all, do not try to fool me, M. de Berault."

But his piercing eyes so disconcerted me that now I had my chance I could not find a word to say, and stood before him mute. I think this pleased him, for his face relaxed.

"Well?" he said at last. "Is that all?"

"The man is not dead," I muttered.

He shrugged his shoulders contemptuously. "What of that?" he said. "That was not what you wanted to say to me."

"Once I saved your Eminence's life," I faltered miserably.

"Admitted," he answered, in his thin, incisive voice. "You mentioned the fact before. On the other hand, you have taken six to my knowledge, M. de Berault. You have lived the life of a bully, a common bravo, a gamester. You, a man of family! For shame! And it has brought you to this. Yet on that one point I am willing to hear more," he added abruptly.

"I might save your Eminence's life again," I cried. It was a sudden inspiration.

"You know something," he said quickly, fixing me with his eyes. "But no," he continued, shaking his head gently. "Pshaw! the trick is old. I have better spies than you, M. de Berault."

"But no better sword," I cried hoarsely. "No, not in all your guard!"

"That is true," he said. "That is true." To my surprise, he spoke in a tone of consideration; and he looked down at the floor. "Let me think, my friend," he continued.

He walked two or three times up and down the room, while I stood trembling. I confess it trembling. The man whose pulses danger has no power to quicken, is seldom proof against suspense; and the sudden hope his words awakened in me so shook me that his figure, as he trod lightly to and fro, with the cat rubbing against his robe and turning time for time with him, wavered before my eyes. I grasped the table to steady myself. I had not admitted even in my own mind how darkly the shadow of Montfaucon and the gallows had fallen across me.

I had leisure to recover myself, for it was some time before he spoke. When he did, it was in a voice harsh, changed, imperative. "You have the reputation of a man faithful, at least, to his employer," he said. "Do not answer me. I say it is so. Well, I will trust you. I will give you one more chance--though it is a desperate one. Woe to you if you fail me! Do you know Cocheforêt in Béarn? It is not far from Auch."

"No, your Eminence."

"Nor M. de Cocheforêt?"

"No, your Eminence."

"So much the better," he retorted. "But you have heard of him. He has been engaged in every Gascon plot since the late King's death, and gave me more trouble last year in the Vivarais than any man twice his years. At present he is at Bosost in Spain, with other refugees, but I have learned that at frequent intervals he visits his wife at Cocheforêt, which is six leagues within the border. On one of these visits he must be arrested."

"That should be easy," I said.

The Cardinal looked at me. "Tush, man! what do you know about it?" he answered bluntly. "It is whispered at Cocheforêt if a soldier crosses the street at Auch. In the house are only two or three servants, but they have the country-side with them to a man, and they are a dangerous breed. A spark might kindle a fresh rising. The arrest, therefore, must be made secretly."

I bowed.

"One resolute man inside the house, with the help of two or three servants whom he could summon to his aid at will, might effect it," the Cardinal continued, glancing at a paper which lay on the table. "The question is, will you be the man, my friend?"

I hesitated; then I bowed. What choice had I?

"Nay, nay, speak out!" he said sharply. "Yes or no, M. de Berault?"

"Yes, your Eminence," I said reluctantly. Again, I say, what choice had I?

"You will bring him to Paris, and alive. He knows things, and that is why I want him. You understand?"

"I understand, Monseigneur," I answered.

"You will get into the house as you can," he continued. "For that you will need strategy, and good strategy. They suspect everybody. You must deceive them. If you fail to deceive them, or, deceiving them, are found out later, M. de Berault--I do not think you will trouble me again, or break the edict a second time. On the other hand, should you deceive me"--he smiled still more subtly, but his voice sank to a purring note--"I will break you on the wheel like the ruined gamester you are!"

I met his look without quailing. "So be it!" I said recklessly. "If I do not bring M. de Cocheforêt to Paris, you may do that to me, and more also!"

"It is a bargain!" he answered slowly. "I think you will be faithful. For money, here are a hundred crowns. That sum should suffice; but if you succeed you shall have twice as much more. Well, that is all, I think. You understand?"

"Yes, Monseigneur."

"Then why do you wait?"

"The lieutenant?" I said modestly.

Monseigneur laughed to himself, and sitting down wrote a word or two on a slip of paper. "Give him that," he said, in high good-humour. "I fear, M. de Berault, you will never get your deserts--in this world!"

AT THE GREEN PILLAR

Cocheforêt lies in a billowy land of oak and beech and chestnut--a land of deep, leafy bottoms, and hills clothed with forest. Ridge and valley, glen and knoll, the woodland, sparsely peopled and more sparsely tilled, stretches away to the great snow mountains that here limit France. It swarms with game--with wolves and bears, deer and boars. To the end of his life I have heard that the great King loved this district, and would sigh, when years and State fell heavily on him, for the beech-groves and box-covered hills of South Béarn. From the terraced steps of Auch you can see the forest roll away in light and shadow, vale and upland, to the base of the snow-peaks; and, though I come from Brittany and love the smell of the salt wind, I have seen few sights that outdo this.

It was the second week in October when I came to Cocheforêt, and, dropping down from the last wooded brow, rode quietly into the place at evening. I was alone, and had ridden all day in a glory of ruddy beech-leaves, through the silence of forest roads, across clear brooks and glades still green. I had seen more of the quiet and peace of the country than had been my share since boyhood, and I felt a little melancholy; it might be for that reason, or because I had no great taste for the task before me--the task now so imminent. In good faith, it was not a gentleman's work, look at it how you might.

But beggars must not be choosers, and I knew that this feeling would pass away. At the inn, in the presence of others, under the spur of necessity, or in the excitement of the chase, were that once begun, I should lose the feeling. When a man is young, he seeks solitude: when he is middle-aged he flies it and his thoughts. I made without ado for the Green Pillar, a little inn in the village street, to which I had been directed at Auch, and, thundering on the door with the knob of my riding-switch, railed at the man for keeping me waiting.

Here and there at hovel doors in the street--which was a mean, poor place, not worthy of the name--men and women looked out at me suspiciously. But I affected to ignore them; and at last the host came. He was a fair-haired man, half Basque, half Frenchman, and had scanned me well, I was sure, through some window or peephole; for, when he came out, he betrayed no surprise at the sight of a well-dressed stranger--a portent in that out-of-the-way village--but eyed me with a kind of sullen reserve.

"I can lie here to-night, I suppose?" I said, dropping the reins on the sorrel's neck. The horse hung its head.

"I don't know," he answered stupidly.

I pointed to the green bough which topped a post that stood opposite the door.

"This is an inn, is it not?" I said.

"Yes," he answered slowly; "it is an inn. But--"

"But you are full, or you are out of food, or your wife is ill, or something else is amiss," I answered peevishly. "All the same, I am going to lie here. So you must make the best of it, and your wife, too--if you have one."

He scratched his head, looking at me with an ugly glitter in his eyes. But he said nothing, and I dismounted.

"Where can I stable my horse?" I asked.

"I'll put it up," he answered sullenly, stepping forward and taking the reins in his hands.

"Very well," I said; "but I go with you. A merciful man is merciful to his beast, and where-ever I go I see my horse fed."

"It will be fed," he said shortly. And then he waited for me to go into the house. "The wife is in there," he continued, looking at me stubbornly.

"Imprimis--if you understand Latin, my friend," I answered, "the horse in the stall."

As if he saw it was no good, he turned the sorrel slowly round, and began to lead it across the village street. There was a shed behind the inn, which I had already marked and taken for the stable, and I was surprised when I found he was not going there. But I made no remark, and in a few minutes saw the horse well stabled in a hovel which seemed to belong to a neighbour.

This done, the man led the way back to the inn, carrying my valise.

"You have no other guests?" I said, with a casual air. I knew he was watching me closely.

"No," he answered.

"This is not much in the way to anywhere, I suppose?"

"No."

That was evident; a more retired place I never saw. The hanging woods, rising steeply to a great height, so shut the valley in that I was puzzled to think how a man could leave it save by the road I had come. The cottages, which were no more than mean, small huts, ran in a straggling double line, with many gaps--through fallen trees and ill-cleared meadows. Among them a noisy brook ran in and out. And the inhabitants--charcoal-burners, or swineherds, or poor people of the like class, were no better than their dwellings. I looked in vain for the Château. It was not to be seen, and I dared not ask for it.

The man led me into the common room of the tavern--a low-roofed, poor place, lacking a chimney or glazed windows, and grimy with smoke and use. The fire--a great half-burned tree--smouldered on a stone hearth, raised a foot from the floor. A huge black pot simmered over it, and beside one window lounged a country fellow talking with the goodwife. In the dusk I could not see his face, but I gave the woman a word, and sat down to wait for my supper.

She seemed more silent than the common run of women; but this might be because her husband was present. While she moved about, getting my meal, he took his place against the doorpost and fell to staring at me so persistently that I felt by no means at my ease. He was a tall, strong fellow, with a rough moustache and brown beard, cut in the mode Henri Quatre; and on the subject of that king--a safe one, I knew, with a Béarnais--and on that alone, I found it possible to make him talk. Even then there was a suspicious gleam in his eyes that bade me abstain from questions; and as the darkness deepened behind him, and the firelight played more and more strongly on his features, and I thought of the leagues of woodland that lay between this remote valley and Auch. I recalled the Cardinal's warning that if I failed in my attempt I should be little likely to trouble Paris again.

The lout by the window paid no attention to me; nor I to him, when I had once satisfied myself that he was really what he seemed to be. But by and by two or three men--rough, uncouth fellows--dropped in to reinforce the landlord, and they, too, seemed to have no other business than to sit in silence looking at me, or now and again to exchange a word in a patois of their own. By the time my supper was ready, the knaves numbered six in all; and, as they were armed to a man with huge Spanish knives, and evidently resented my presence in their dull rustic fashion--every rustic is suspicious-- I began to think that, unwittingly, I had put my head into a wasp's nest.

Nevertheless, I ate and drank with apparent appetite; but little that passed within the circle of light cast by the smoky lamp escaped me. I watched the men's looks and gestures at least as sharply as they watched mine; and all the time I was racking my wits for some mode of disarming their suspicions--or failing that, of learning something more of the position, which, it was clear, far exceeded in difficulty and danger anything I had expected. The whole valley, it would seem, was on the lookout to protect my man!

I had purposely brought with me from Auch a couple of bottles of choice Armagnac; and these had been carried into the house with my saddlebags. I took one out now and opened it, and carelessly offered a dram of the spirit to the landlord. He took it. As he drank it, I saw his face flush; he handed back the cup reluctantly, and on that hint I offered him another. The strong spirit was already beginning to work. He accepted, and in a few minutes began to talk more freely and with less of the constraint which had marked us. Still, his tongue ran chiefly on questions--he would know this, he would learn that; but even this was a welcome change. I told him openly whence I had come, by what road, how long I had stayed in Auch, and where; and so far I satisfied his curiosity. Only when I came to the subject of my visit to Cocheforêt I kept a mysterious silence, hinting darkly at business in Spain and friends across the border, and this and that, and giving the peasants to understand, if they pleased, that I was in the same interest as their exiled master.

They took the bait, winked at one another, and began to look at me in a more friendly way--the landlord foremost. But when I had led them so far, I dared go no farther, lest I should commit myself and be found out. I stopped, therefore, and, harking back to general subjects, chanced to compare my province with theirs. The landlord, now become almost talkative, was not slow to take up this challenge; and it presently led to my acquiring a curious piece of knowledge. He was boasting of his great snow mountains, the forests that propped them, the bears that roamed in them, the izards that loved the ice, and the boars that fed on the oak mast.

"Well," I said, quite by chance, "we have not these things, it is true. But we have things in the north you have not. We have tens of thousands of good horses--not such ponies as you breed here. At the horse fair at Fécamp my sorrel would be lost in the crowd. Here in the south you will not meet his match in a long day's journey."

"Do not make too sure of that!" the man replied, his eyes bright with triumph and the dram. "What would you say if I showed you a better--in my own stable?"

I saw that his words sent a kind of thrill through his other hearers, and that such of them as understood--for two or three of them talked their patois only--looked at him angrily; and in a twinkling I began to comprehend. But I affected dulness, and laughed scornfully.

"Seeing is believing," I said. "I doubt if you know a good horse here when you see one, my friend."

"Oh, don't I?" he said, winking. "Indeed!"

"I doubt it," I answered stubbornly.

"Then come with me, and I will show you one," he retorted, discretion giving way to vainglory. His wife and the others, I saw, looked at him dumbfounded; but, without paying any heed to them, he took up a lanthorn, and, assuming an air of peculiar wisdom, opened the door. "Come with me," he continued. "I don't know a good horse when I see one, don't I? I know a better than yours, at any rate!"

I should not have been surprised if the other men had interfered; but--I suppose he was a leader among them, and they did not, and in a moment we were outside. Three paces through the darkness took us to the stable, an offset at the back of the inn. My man twirled the pin, and, leading the way in, raised his lanthorn. A horse whinnied softly, and turned its bright, soft eyes on us--a baldfaced chestnut, with white hairs in its tail and one white stocking.

"There!" my guide exclaimed, waving the lanthorn to and fro boastfully, that I might see its points. "What do you say to that? Is that an undersized pony?"

"No," I answered, purposely stinting my praise. "It is pretty fair--for this country."

"Or any country," he answered wrathfully. "Any country, I say--I don't care where it is! And I have reason to know! Why, man, that horse is-- But there, that is a good horse, if ever you saw one!" And with that he ended abruptly and lamely, lowering the lanthorn with a sudden gesture, and turning to the door. He was on the instant in such hurry, that he almost shouldered me out.

But I understood. I knew that he had nearly betrayed all--that he had been on the point of blurting out that that was M. de Cocheforêt's horse! M. de Cocheforêt's, comprenez bien! And while I turned away my face in the darkness, that he might not see me smile, I was not surprised to find the man in a moment changed, and become, in the closing of the door, as sober and suspicious as before, ashamed of himself and enraged with me, and in a mood to cut my throat for a trifle.

It was not my cue to quarrel, however--anything but that. I made, therefore, as if I had seen nothing, and when we were back in the inn praised the horse grudgingly, and like a man but half convinced. The ugly looks and ugly weapons I saw around me were fine incentives to caution; and no Italian, I flatter myself, could have played his part more nicely than I did. But I was heartily glad when it was over, and I found myself, at last, left alone for the night in a little garret--a mere fowl-house--upstairs, formed by the roof and gable walls, and hung with strings of apples and chestnuts. It was a poor sleeping-place--rough, chilly, and unclean. I ascended to it by a ladder; my cloak and a little fern formed my only bed. But I was glad to accept it. It enabled me to be alone and to think out the position unwatched.

Of course M. de Cocheforêt was at the Château. He had left his horse here, and gone up on foot: probably that was his usual plan. He was therefore within my reach, in one sense--I could not have come at a better time--but in another he was as much beyond it as if I were still in Paris. So far was I from being able to seize him that I dared not ask a question or let fall a rash word, or even look about me freely. I saw I dared not. The slightest hint of my mission, the faintest breath of distrust, would lead to throat-cutting--and the throat would be mine; while the longer I lay in the village, the greater suspicion I should incur, and the closer would be the watch kept over me.

In such a position some men might have given up the attempt and saved themselves across the border. But I have always valued myself on my fidelity, and I did not shrink. If not to-day, to-morrow; if not this time, next time. The dice do not always turn up aces. Bracing myself, therefore, to the occasion, I crept, as soon as the house was quiet, to the window, a small, square, open lattice, much cobwebbed, and partly stuffed with hay. I looked out. The village seemed to be asleep. The dark branches of trees hung a few feet away, and almost obscured a grey, cloudy sky, through which a wet moon sailed drearily. Looking downwards, I could at first see nothing; but as my eyes grew used to the darkness--I had only just put out my rushlight-- I made out the stable-door and the shadowy outlines of the lean-to roof.

I had hoped for this. I could now keep watch, and learn at least whether Cocheforêt left before morning. If he did not I should know he was still here. If he did, I should be the better for seeing his features, and learning, perhaps, other things that might be of use.

Making up my mind to be uncomfortable, I sat down on the floor by the lattice, and began a vigil that might last, I knew, until morning. It did last about an hour. At the end of that time I heard whispering below, then footsteps; then, as some persons turned a corner, a voice speaking aloud and carelessly. I could not catch the words spoken; but the voice was a gentleman's, and its bold accents and masterful tone left me in no doubt that the speaker was M. de Cocheforêt himself. Hoping to learn more, I pressed my face nearer to the opening, and I had just made out through the gloom two figures--one that of a tall, slight man, wearing a cloak, the other, I thought, a woman's, in a sheeny white dress--when a thundering rap on the door of my garret made me spring back a yard from the lattice, and lie down hurriedly on my couch. The noise was repeated.

"Well?" I cried, cursing the untimely interruption. I was burning with anxiety to see more. "What is it? What is the matter?"

The trapdoor was lifted a foot or more. The landlord thrust up his head.

"You called, did you not?" he asked. He held up a rushlight, which illumined half the room and lit up his grinning face.

"Called--at this hour of the night, you fool?" I answered angrily. "No! I did not call. Go to bed, man!"

But he remained on the ladder, gaping stupidly.

"I heard you," he said.

"Go to bed! You are drunk!" I answered, sitting up. "I tell you I did not call."

"Oh, very well," he answered slowly. "And you do not want anything?"

"Nothing--except to be left alone!" I replied sourly.

"Umph!" he said. "Good-night!"

"Good-night! Good-night!" I answered, with what patience I might. The tramp of the horse's hoofs as it was led out of the stable was in my ear at the moment. "Good-night!" I continued feverishly, hoping he would still retire in time, and I have a chance to look out. "I want to sleep."

"Good," he said, with a broad grin. "But it is early yet, and you have plenty of time." And then, at last, he slowly let down the trapdoor, and I heard him chuckle as he went down the ladder.

Before he reached the bottom I was at the window. The woman whom I had seen still stood below, in the same place; and beside her a man in a peasant's dress, holding a lanthorn, But the man, the man I wanted to see was no longer there. And it was evident that he was gone; it was evident that the others no longer feared me, for while I gazed the landlord came out to them with another lanthorn, and said something to the lady, and she looked up at my window and laughed.

It was a warm night, and she wore nothing over her white dress. I could see her tall, shapely figure and shining eyes, and the firm contour of her beautiful face; which, if any fault might be found with it, erred in being too regular. She looked like a woman formed by nature to meet dangers and difficulties; and even here, at midnight, in the midst of these desperate men, she seemed in place. It was possible that under her queenly exterior, and behind the contemptuous laugh with which she heard the land lord's story, there lurked a woman's soul capable of folly and tenderness. But no outward sign betrayed its presence.

I scanned her very carefully; and secretly, if the truth be told, I was glad to find Madame de Cocheforêt such a woman. I was glad that she had laughed as she had--that she was not a little, tender, child-like woman, to be crushed by the first pinch of trouble. For if I succeeded in my task, if I--but, pish! Women, I said, were all alike. She would find consolation quickly enough.

I watched until the group broke up, and Madame, with one of the men, went her way round the corner of the inn, and out of my sight. Then I retired to bed again, feeling more than ever perplexed what course I should adopt. It was clear that, to succeed, I must obtain admission to the house. This was garrisoned, unless my instructions erred, by two or three old men-servants only, and as many women; since Madame, to disguise her husband's visits the more easily, lived, and gave out that she lived, in great retirement. To seize her husband at home, therefore, might be no impossible task; though here, in the heart of the village, a troop of horse might make the attempt, and fail.

But how was I to gain admission to the house--a house guarded by quick-witted women, and hedged in with all the precautions love could devise? That was the question; and dawn found me still debating it, still as far as ever from an answer. With the first light I was glad to get up. I thought that the fresh air might inspire me, and I was tired, besides, of my stuffy closet. I crept stealthily down the ladder, and managed to pass unseen through the lower room, in which several persons were snoring heavily. The outer door was not fastened, and in a hand-turn I stood in the street.

It was still so early that the trees stood up black against the reddening sky, but the bough upon the post before the door was growing green, and in a few minutes the grey light would be everywhere. Already even in the road way there was a glimmering of it; and as I stood at the corner of the house--where I could command both the front and the side on which the stable opened--looking greedily for any trace of the midnight departure, my eyes detected something light-coloured lying on the ground. It was not more than two or three paces from me, and I stepped to it and picked it up curiously, hoping it might be a note. It was not a note, however, but a tiny orange-coloured sachet, such as women carry in the bosom. It was full of some faintly scented powder, and bore on one side the initial "E," worked in white silk; and was altogether a dainty little toy, such as women love.

Doubtless Madame de Cocheforêt had dropped it in the night. I turned it over and over; and then I put it away with a smile, thinking it might be useful some time, and in some way. I had scarcely done this, and turned with the intention of exploring the street, when the door behind me creaked on its leather hinges, and in a moment my host stood at my elbow.

Evidently his suspicions were again aroused, for from that time he managed to be with me, on one pretence or another, until noon. Moreover, his manner grew each moment more churlish, his hints plainer; until I could scarcely avoid noticing the one or the other. About midday, having followed me for the twentieth time into the street, he came at last to the point, by asking me rudely if I did not need my horse.

"No," I said. "Why do you ask?"

"Because," he answered, with an ugly smile, "this is not a very healthy place for strangers."

"Ah!" I retorted. "But the border air suits me, you see."

It was a lucky answer; for, taken with my talk of the night before, it puzzled him, by again suggesting that I was on the losing side, and had my reasons for lying near Spain. Before he had done scratching his head over it, the clatter of hoofs broke the sleepy quiet of the village street, and the lady I had seen the night before rode quickly round the corner, and drew her horse on to its haunches. Without looking at me, she called to the innkeeper to come to her stirrup.

He went. The moment his back was turned, I slipped away, and in a twinkling was hidden by a house. Two or three glum-looking fellows stared at me as I passed, but no one moved; and in two minutes I was clear of the village, and in a half-worn track which ran through the wood, and led--if my ideas were right--to the Château. To discover the house and learn all that was to be learned about its situation was my most pressing need: even at the risk of a knife-thrust, I was determined to satisfy it.

I had not gone two hundred paces along the path before I heard the tread of a horse behind me, and I had just time to hide myself before Madame came up and rode by me, sitting her horse gracefully, and with all the courage of a northern woman. I watched her pass, and then, assured by her presence that I was in the right road, I hurried after her. Two minutes' walking at speed brought me to a light wooden bridge spanning a stream. I crossed this, and, the wood opening, saw before me first a wide, pleasant meadow, and beyond this a terrace. On the terrace, pressed upon on three sides by thick woods, stood a grey mansion, with the corner tourelles, steep, high roofs, and round balconies that men loved and built in the days of the first Francis.

It was of good size, but wore, I fancied, a gloomy aspect. A great yew hedge, which seemed to enclose a walk or bowling-green, hid the ground floor of the east wing from view, while a formal rose garden, stiff even in neglect, lay in front of the main building. The west wing, whose lower roofs fell gradually away to the woods, probably contained the stables and granaries.

I stood a moment only, but I marked all, and noted how the road reached the house, and which windows were open to attack; then I turned and hastened back. Fortunately, I met no one between the house and the village, and was able to enter the inn with an air of the most complete innocence.

Short as had been my absence, I found things altered there. Round the door loitered and chattered three strangers--stout, well-armed fellows, whose bearing suggested a curious mixture of smugness and independence. Half-a-dozen pack-horses stood tethered to the post in front of the house; and the landlord's manner, from being rude and churlish only, had grown perplexed and almost timid. One of the strangers, I soon found, supplied him with wine; the others were travelling merchants, who rode in the first one's company for the sake of safety. All were substantial men from Tarbes--solid burgesses; and I was not long in guessing that my host, fearing what might leak out before them, and particularly that I might refer to the previous night's disturbance, was on tenterhooks while they remained.

For a time this did not suggest anything to me. But when we had all taken our seats for supper there came an addition to the party. The door opened, and the fellow whom I had seen the night before with Madame de

Cocheforêt entered, and took a stool by the fire. I felt sure that he was one of the servants at the Château; and in a flash his presence inspired me with the most feasible plan for obtaining admission which I had yet hit upon. I felt myself growing hot at the thought--it seemed so full of promise and of danger--and on the instant, without giving myself time to think too much, I began to carry it into effect.

I called for two or three bottles of better wine, and, assuming a jovial air, passed it round the table. When we had drunk a few glasses, I fell to talking, and, choosing politics, took the side of the Languedoc party and the malcontents, in so reckless a fashion that the innkeeper was beside himself at my imprudence. The merchants, who belonged to the class with whom the Cardinal was always most popular, looked first astonished and then enraged. But I was not to be checked. Hints and sour looks were lost upon me. I grew more outspoken with every glass, I drank to the Rochellois, I swore it would not be long before they raised their heads again; and at last, while the innkeeper and his wife were engaged lighting the lamp, I passed round the bottle and called on all for a toast.

"I'll give you one to begin," I bragged noisily. "A gentleman's toast! A southern toast! Here is confusion to the Cardinal, and a health to all who hate him!"

"Mon Dieu!" one of the strangers cried, springing from his seat in a rage. "I am not going to stomach that! Is your house a common treason-hole," he continued, turning furiously on the landlord, "that you suffer this?"

"Hoity-toity!" I answered, coolly keeping my seat. "What is all this? Don't you relish my toast, little man?"

"No--nor you!" he retorted hotly, "whoever you may be!"

"Then I will give you another," I answered, with a hiccough. "Perhaps it will be more to your taste. Here is the Duke of Orleans, and may he soon be King!"

THE HOUSE IN THE WOOD

MY words fairly startled the three men out of their anger. For a moment they glared at me as if they had seen a ghost. Then the wine-merchant clapped his hand on the table. "That is enough!" he said, with a look at his companions. "I think there can be no mistake about that. As damnable treason as ever I heard whispered! I congratulate you, Sir, on your boldness. As for you," he continued, turning with an ugly sneer to the landlord, "I shall know now the company you keep! I was not aware that my wine wet whistles to such a tune!"

But if he was startled, the innkeeper was furious, seeing his character thus taken away; and, being at no time a man of many words, he vented his rage exactly in the way I wished. In a twinkling he raised such an uproar as can scarcely be conceived. With a roar like a bull's he ran headlong at the table, and overturned it on the top of me. The woman saved the lamp and fled with it into a corner, whence she and the man from the Château watched the skirmish in silence; but the pewter cups and platters flew spinning across the floor, while the table pinned me to the ground among the ruins of my stool. Having me at this disadvantage--for at first I made no resistance--the landlord began to belabour me with the first thing he snatched up, and when I tried to defend myself cursed me with each blow for a treacherous rogue and a vagrant. Meanwhile, the three merchants, delighted with the turn things had taken, skipped round us laughing; and now hounded him on, now bantered me with "How is that for the Duke of Orleans?" and "How now, traitor?"

When I thought this had lasted long enough--or, to speak more plainly, when I could stand the innkeeper's drubbing no longer--I threw him off by a great effort, and struggled to my feet. But still, though the blood was trickling down my face, I refrained from drawing my sword. I caught up instead a leg of the stool which lay handy, and, watching my opportunity, dealt the landlord a shrewd blow under the ear, which laid him out in a moment on the wreck of his own table.

"Now!" I cried, brandishing my new weapon, which fitted the hand to a nicety, "come on! Come on, if you dare to strike a blow, you peddling, truckling, huckstering knaves! A fig for you and your shaveling Cardinal!"

The red-faced wine-merchant drew his sword in a one-two. "Why, you drunken fool," he said wrathfully, "put that stick down, or I will spit you like a lark!"

"Lark in your teeth!" I cried, staggering as if the wine were in my head. "Another word, and I--"

He made a couple of savage passes at me, but in a twinkling his sword flew across the room.

"Voilà!" I shouted, lurching forward, as if I had luck and not skill to thank for it. "Now the next! Come on, come on--you white-livered knaves!" And, pretending a drunken frenzy, I flung my weapon bodily amongst them, and seizing the nearest, began to wrestle with him.

In a moment they all threw themselves upon me, and, swearing copiously, bore me back to the door. The wine-merchant cried breathlessly to the woman to open it, and in a twinkling they had me through it and half way across the road. The one thing I feared was a knife-thrust in the mêlée; but I had to run that risk, and the men were honest enough and, thinking me drunk, indulgent. In a trice I found myself on my back in the dirt, with my head humming; and heard the bars of the door fall noisily into their places.

I got up and went to the door, and, to play out my part, hammered on it frantically, crying out to them to let me in. But the three travellers only jeered at me, and the landlord, coming to the window, with his head bleeding, shook his fist at me and cursed me for a mischief-maker.

Baffled in this I retired to a log which lay in the road a few paces from the house, and sat down on it to await events. With torn clothes and bleeding face, hatless and covered with dirt, I was in scarcely better case than my opponent. It was raining, too, and the dripping branches swayed over my head. The wind was in the south--the coldest quarter. I began to feel chilled and dispirited. If my scheme failed, I had forfeited roof and bed to no purpose, and placed future progress out of the question. It was a critical moment.

But at last that happened for which I had been looking. The door swung open a few inches, and a man came noiselessly out; the door was quickly barred behind him. He stood a moment, waiting on the threshold and peering into the gloom; and seemed to expect to be attacked. Finding himself unmolested, however, and all quiet, he went off steadily down the street--towards the Château.

I let a couple of minutes go by and then I followed. I had no difficulty in hitting on the track at the end of the street, but when I had once plunged into the wood, I found myself in darkness so intense that I soon strayed from the path, and fell over roots, and tore my clothes with thorns, and lost my temper twenty times before I found the path again. However, I gained the bridge at last, and caught sight of a light twinkling before me. To make for it across the meadow and terrace was an easy task; yet when I had reached the door and had hammered upon it, I was in so sorry a plight that I sank down, and had no need to play a part or pretend to be worse than I was.

For a long time no one answered. The dark house towering above me remained silent. I could hear, mingled with the throbbings of my heart, the steady croaking of the frogs in a pond near the stables; but no other sound. In a frenzy of impatience and disgust I stood up again and hammered, kicking with my heels on the nail-studded door, and crying out desperately, "A moi! A moi!"

Then, or a moment later, I heard a remote door opened; footsteps as of more than one person drew near. I raised my voice and cried again, "A moi!"

"Who is there?" a voice asked.

"A gentleman in distress," I answered piteously, moving my hands across the door. "For God's sake open and let me in. I am hurt, and dying of cold."

"What brings you here?" the voice asked sharply. Despite its tartness, I fancied it was a woman's.

"Heaven knows!" I answered desperately. "I cannot tell. They maltreated me at the inn, and threw me into the street. I crawled away, and have been wandering in the wood for hours. Then I saw a light here."

Thereon, some muttering took place on the other side of the door, to which I had my ear. It ended in the bars being lowered. The door swung partly open and a light shone out, dazzling me. I tried to shade my eyes with my fingers, and as I did so fancied I heard a murmur of pity. But when I looked in under screen of my hand I saw only one person--the man who held the light, and his aspect was so strange, so terrifying, that, shaken as I was by fatigue, I recoiled a step.

He was a tall and very thin man, meanly dressed in a short scanty jacket and well-darned hose. Unable, for some reason, to bend his neck, he carried his head with a strange stiffness.

And that head! Never did living man show a face so like death. His forehead was bald and white, his cheek-bones stood out under the strained skin, all the lower part of his face fell in, his jaws receded, his cheeks were hollow, his lips and chin were thin and fleshless. He seemed to have only one expression--a fixed grin.

While I stood looking at this formidable creature he made a quick motion to shut the door again, smiling more widely. I had the presence of mind to thrust in my foot, and, before he could resent the act, a voice in the background cried: "For shame, Clon! Stand back. Stand back, do you hear? I am afraid, Monsieur, that you are hurt."

The last words were my welcome to that house; and, spoken at an hour and in circumstances so gloomy, they made a lasting impression. Round the hall ran a gallery, and this, the height of the apartment, and the dark panelling seemed to swallow up the light. I stood within the entrance (as it seemed to me) of a huge cave; the skull-headed porter had the air of an ogre. Only the voice which greeted me dispelled the illusion. I turned trembling towards the quarter whence it came, and, shading my eyes, made out a woman's form standing in a doorway under the gallery. A second figure, which I took to be that of the servant I had seen at the inn, loomed uncertainly beside her.

I bowed in silence. My teeth were chattering I was faint without feigning, and felt a kind of terror, hard to explain, at the sound of this woman's voice.

"One of our people has told me about you," she continued, speaking out of the darkness. "I am sorry that this has happened to you here, but I am afraid that you were indiscreet."

"I take all the blame, Madame," I answered humbly. "I ask only shelter for the night."

"The time has not yet come when we cannot give our friends that!" she answered, with noble courtesy. "When it does, Monsieur, we shall be homeless ourselves."

I shivered, looking anywhere but at her; for I had not sufficiently pictured this scene of my arrival--I had not foreseen its details; and now I took part in it I felt a miserable meanness weigh me down. I had never from the first liked the work! But, I had had no choice. And I had no choice now. Luckily, the guise in which I came, my fatigue, and wound were a sufficient mark, or I should have incurred suspicion at once. For I am sure that if ever in this world a brave man wore a hang-dog air, or Gil de Berault fell below himself, it was then and there--on Madame de Cocheforêt's threshold, with her welcome sounding in my ears.

One, I think, did suspect me. Clon, the porter, continued to hold the door obstinately ajar and to eye me with grinning spite, until his mistress, with some sharpness, bade him drop the bars, and conduct me to a room.

"Do you go also, Louis," she continued, speaking to the man beside her, "and see this gentleman comfortably disposed. I am sorry," she added, addressing me in the graceful tone she had before used, and I thought I could see her head bend in the darkness, "that our present circumstances do not permit us to welcome you more fitly, Monsieur. But the troubles of the times--however, you will excuse what is lacking. Until to-morrow, I have the honour to bid you goodnight."

"Good-night, Madame," I stammered, trembling. I had not been able to distinguish her face in the gloom of the doorway, but her voice, her greeting, her presence, unmanned me. I was troubled and perplexed; I had not spirit to kick a dog. I followed the two servants from the hall without heeding how we went; nor was it until we came to a full stop at a door in a whitewashed corridor, and it was forced upon me that something was in question between my two conductors, that I began to take notice.

Then I saw that one of them, Louis, wished to lodge me here where we stood. The porter, on the other hand, who held the keys, would not. He did not speak a word, nor did the other--and this gave a queer ominous character to the debate; but he continued to jerk his head towards the farther end of the corridor, and, at last, he carried his point. Louis shrugged his shoulders, and moved on, glancing askance at me; and I, not understanding the matter in debate, followed the pair in silence.

We reached the end of the corridor, and there, for an instant, the monster with the keys paused and grinned at me. Then he turned into a narrow passage on the left, and after following it for some paces, halted before a small, strong door. His key jarred in the lock, but he forced it shrieking round, and with a savage flourish threw the door open.

I walked in and saw a mean, bare chamber with barred windows. The floor was indifferently clean, there was no furniture. The yellow light of the lanthorn falling on the stained walls gave the place the look of a dungeon. I turned to the two men. "This is not a very good room," I said. "And it feels damp. Have you no other?"

Louis looked doubtfully at his companion. But the porter shook his head stubbornly.

"Why does he not speak?" I asked with impatience.

"He is dumb," Louis answered.

"Dumb!" I exclaimed. "But he hears."

"He has ears," the servant answered drily. "But he has no tongue, Monsieur."

I shuddered. "How did he lose it?" I asked.

"At Rochelle. He was a spy, and the King's people took him the day the town surrendered. They spared his life, but cut out his tongue."

"Ah!" I said. I wished to say more, to be natural, to show myself at my ease. But the porter's eyes seemed to burn into me, and my own tongue clove to the roof of my mouth. He opened his lips and pointed to his throat with a horrid gesture, and I shook my head and turned from him-- "You can let me have some bedding?" I murmured hastily, for the sake of saying something, and to escape.

"Of course, Monsieur," Louis answered. "I will fetch some."

He went away, thinking doubtless that Clon would stay with me. But after waiting a minute the porter strode off also with the lanthorn, leaving me to stand in the middle of the damp, dark room, and reflect on the position. It was plain that Clon suspected me. This prison-like room, with its barred window at the back of the house, and in the wing farthest from the stables, proved so much. Clearly, he was a dangerous fellow, of whom I must beware. I had just begun to wonder how Madame could keep such a monster in her house, when I heard his step returning. He came in, lighting Louis, who carried a small pallet and a bundle of coverings.

The dumb man had, besides the lanthorn, a bowl of water and a piece of rag in his hand. He set them down, and going out again, fetched in a stool. Then he hung up the lanthorn on a nail, took the bowl and rag, and invited me to sit down.

I was loth to let him touch me; but he continued to stand over me, pointing and grinning with dark persistence, and, rather than stand on a trifle, I sat down at last, and gave him his way. He bathed my head carefully enough, and I dare say did it good; but I understood. I knew that his only desire was to learn whether the cut was real or a pretence. I began to fear him more and more, and, until he was gone from the room, dared scarcely lift my face, lest he should read too much in it.

Alone, even, I felt uncomfortable. This seemed so sinister a business, and so ill begun. I was in the house. But Madame's frank voice haunted me, and the dumb man's eyes, full of suspicion and menace. When I presently got up and tried my door, I found it locked. The room smelled dank and close--like a vault. I could not see through the barred window; but I could hear the boughs sweep it in ghostly fashion; and I guessed that it looked out where the wood grew close to the walls of the house; and that even in the day the sun never peeped through it.

Nevertheless, tired and worn out, I slept at last. When I awoke the room was full of grey light, the door stood open, and Louis, looking ashamed of himself, waited by my pallet with a cup of wine in his hand, and some bread and fruit on a platter.

"Will Monsieur be good enough to rise?" he said. "It is eight o'clock."

"Willingly," I answered tartly. "Now that the door is unlocked."

He turned red. "It was an oversight," he stammered. "Clon is accustomed to lock the door, and he did it inadvertently, forgetting that there was any one--"

"Inside!" I said drily.

"Precisely, Monsieur."

"Ah!" I replied. "Well, I do not think the oversight would please Madame de Cocheforêt, if she heard of it?"

"If Monsieur would have the kindness not to--"

"Mention it, my good fellow?" I answered, looking at him with meaning, as I rose. "No; but it must not occur again."

I saw that this man was not like Clon. He had the instincts of the family servant, and freed from the influences of darkness, felt ashamed of his conduct. While he arranged my clothes, he looked round the room with an air of distaste, and muttered once or twice that the furniture of the principal chambers was packed away.

"M. de Cocheforêt is abroad, I think?" I said, as I dressed.

"And likely to remain there," the man answered carelessly, shrugging his shoulders. "Monsieur will doubtless have heard that he is in trouble. In the meantime, the house is triste, and Monsieur must overlook much, if he stays. Madame lives retired, and the roads are ill-made and visitors few."

"When the lion was ill the jackals left him," I said.

Louis nodded. "It is true," he answered simply. He made no boast or brag on his own account, I noticed; and it came home to me that he was a faithful fellow, such as I love. I questioned him discreetly, and learned that he and Clon and an older man who lived over the stables were the only male servants left of a great household. Madame, her sister-in-law, and three women completed the family.

It took me some time to repair my wardrobe, so that I dare say it was nearly ten when I left my dismal little room. I found Louis waiting in the corridor, and he told me that Madame de Cocheforêt and Mademoiselle were in the rose-garden, and would be pleased to receive me. I nodded, and he guided me through several dim passages to a parlour with an open door, through which the sun shone in gaily. Cheered by the morning air and this sudden change to pleasantness and life, I stepped lightly out.

The two ladies were walking up and down a wide path which bisected the garden. The weeds grew rankly in the gravel underfoot, the rose-bushes which bordered the walk thrust their branches here and there in untrained freedom, a dark yew hedge which formed the background bristled with rough shoots and sadly needed trimming. But I did not see any of these things then. The grace, the noble air, the distinction of the two women who paced slowly to meet me--and who shared all these qualities greatly as they differed in others--left me no power to notice trifles.

Mademoiselle was a head shorter than her belle sœur--a slender woman and petite, with a beautiful face and a fair complexion. She walked with dignity, but beside Madame's stately figure she seemed almost childish. And it was characteristic of the two that Mademoiselle as they drew near to me regarded me with sorrowful attention, Madame with a grave smile.

I bowed low. They returned the salute. "This is my sister," Madame de Cocheforêt said, with a slight, a very slight air of condescension. "Will you please to tell me your name, Monsieur?"

"I am M. de Barthe, a gentleman of Normandy," I said, taking the name of my mother. My own, by a possibility, might be known.

Madame's face wore a puzzled look. "I do not know your name, I think," she said thoughtfully. Doubtless she was going over in her mind all the names with which conspiracy had made her familiar.

"That is my misfortune, Madame," I said humbly.

"Nevertheless I am going to scold you," she rejoined, still eyeing me with some keenness. "I am glad to see that you are none the worse for your adventure--but others may be. And you should have borne that in mind."

"I do not think that I hurt the man seriously," I stammered.

"I do not refer to that," she answered coldly. "You know, or should know, that we are in disgrace here; that the Government regards us already with an evil eye, and that a very small thing would lead them to garrison the village and perhaps oust us from the little the wars have left us. You should have known this and considered it," she continued. "Whereas--I do not say that you are a braggart, M. de Barthe. But on this one occasion you seem to have played the part of one."

"Madame, I did not think," I stammered.

"Want of thought causes much evil," she answered, smiling. "However, I have spoken, and we trust that while you stay with us you will be more careful. For the rest, Monsieur," she continued graciously, raising her hand to prevent me speaking, "we do not know why you are here, or what plans you are pursuing. And we do not wish to know. It is enough that you are of our side. This house is at your service as long as you please to use it. And if we can aid you in any other way we will do so."

"Madame!" I exclaimed; and there I stopped. I could not say any more. The rose-garden, with its air of neglect, the shadow of the quiet house that fell across it, the great yew hedge which backed it, and was the pattern of one under which I had played in childhood--all had points that pricked me. But the women's kindness, their unquestioning confidence, the noble air of hospitality which moved them! Against these and their placid beauty in its peaceful frame I had no shield. I turned away, and feigned to be overcome by gratitude. "I have no words--to thank you!" I muttered presently. "I am a little shaken this morning. I--pardon me."

"We will leave you for a while," Mademoiselle de Cocheforêt said, in gentle, pitying tones. "The air will revive you. Louis shall call you when we go to dinner, M. de Barthe. Come, Elise."

I bowed low to hide my face, and they nodded pleasantly--not looking closely at me--as they walked by me to the house. I watched the two gracious, pale-robed figures until the doorway swallowed them, and then I walked away to a quiet corner where the shrubs grew highest and the yew hedge threw its deepest shadow, and I stood to think.

They were strange thoughts, I remember. If the oak can think at the moment the wind uproots it, or the gnarled thorn-bush when the landslip tears it from the slope, they may have such thoughts. I stared at the leaves, at the rotting blossoms, into the dark cavities of the hedge; I stared mechanically, dazed and wondering. What was the purpose for which I was here? What was the work I had come to do? Above all, how--my God! how was I to do it in the face of these helpless women, who trusted me--who opened their house to me? Clon had not frightened me, nor the loneliness of the leagued village, nor the remoteness of this corner where the dread Cardinal seemed a name, and the King's writ ran slowly, and the rebellion, long quenched elsewhere, still smouldered. But Madame's pure faith, the younger woman's tenderness--how was I to face these?

I cursed the Cardinal, I cursed the English fool who had brought me to this, I cursed the years of plenty and scarceness and the Quartier Marais, and Zaton's, where I had lived like a pig, and--

A touch fell on my arm. I turned. It was Clon. How he had stolen up so quietly, how long he had been at my elbow, I could not tell. But his eyes gleamed spitefully in their deep sockets, and he laughed with his fleshless lips; and I hated him. In the daylight the man looked more like a death's-head than ever. I fancied I read in his face that he knew my secret, and I flashed into rage at sight of him.

"What is it?" I cried, with another oath. "Don't lay your corpse-claws on me!"

He mowed at me, and, bowing with ironical politeness, pointed to the house. "Is Madame served?" I said impatiently, crushing down my anger. "Is that what you mean, fool?"

He nodded.

"Very well," I retorted. "I can find my way, then. You may go!"

He fell behind, and I strode back through the sunshine and flowers, and along the grass-grown paths, to the door by which I had come. I walked fast, but his shadow kept pace with me, driving out the strange thoughts in which I had been indulging. Slowly but surely it darkened my mood. After all, this was a little, little place; the people who lived here--I shrugged my shoulders. France, power, pleasure, life lay yonder in the great city. A boy might wreck himself here for a fancy; a man of the world, never. When I entered the room, where the two ladies stood waiting for me by the table, I was myself again.

"Clon made you understand, then?" the younger woman said kindly.

"Yes, Mademoiselle," I answered. On which I saw the two smile at one another, and I added: "He is a strange creature. I wonder you can bear to have him near you."

"Poor man! You do not know his story?" Madame said.

"I have heard something of it," I answered. "Louis told me."

"Well, I do shudder at him, sometimes," she replied, in a low voice. "He has suffered--and horribly, and for us. But I wish it had been on any other service. Spies are necessary things, but one does not wish to have to do with them! Anything in the nature of treachery is so horrible."

"Quick, Louis! the cognac, if you have any there!" Mademoiselle exclaimed. "I am sure you are--still feeling ill, Monsieur."

"No, I thank you," I muttered hoarsely, making an effort to recover myself. "I am quite well. It was an old wound that sometimes touches me."

MADAME AND MADEMOISELLE

To be frank, however, it was not the old wound that touched me so nearly, but Madame's words; which, finishing what Clon's sudden appearance in the garden had begun, went a long way towards hardening me and throwing me back into myself. I saw with bitterness--what I had perhaps forgotten for a moment--how great was the chasm which separated me from these women; how impossible it was we could long think alike; how far apart in views, in experience, in aims we were. And while I made a mock in my heart of their high-flown sentiments--or thought I did--I laughed no less at the folly which had led me to dream, even for a moment, that I could, at my age, go back--go back and risk all for a whim, a scruple, the fancy of a lonely hour.

I dare say something of this showed in my face: for Madame's eyes mirrored a dim reflection of trouble as she looked at me, and Mademoiselle ate nervously and at random. At any rate, I fancied so, and I hastened to compose myself; and the two, in pressing upon me the simple dainties of the table, soon forgot, or appeared to forget, the incident.

Yet in spite of this contretemps, that first meal had a strange charm for me. The round table whereat we dined was spread inside the open door which led to the garden, so that the October sunshine fell full on the spotless linen and quaint old plate, and the fresh balmy air filled the room with the scent of sweet herbs. Louis served us with the mien of major-domo, and set on each dish as though it had been a peacock or a mess of ortolans. The woods provided the larger portion of our meal; the garden did its part; the confections Mademoiselle had cooked with her own hand.

By-and-bye, as the meal went on, as Louis trod to and fro across the polished floor, and the last insects of summer hummed sleepily outside, and the two gracious faces continued to smile at me out of the gloom--for the ladies sat with their backs to the door--I began to dream again. I began to sink again into folly--that was half pleasure, half pain. The fury of the gaming-house and the riot of Zaton's seemed far away. The triumphs of the fencing-room--even they grew cheap and tawdry. I thought of existence as one outside it. I balanced this against that, and wondered whether, after all, the red soutane were so much better than the homely jerkin, or the fame of a day than ease and safety.

And life at Cocheforêt was all after the pattern of this dinner. Each day, I might almost say each meal, gave rise to the same sequence of thoughts. In Clon's presence, or when some word of Madame's, unconsciously harsh, reminded me of the distance between us, I was myself. At other times, in face of this peaceful and intimate life, which was only rendered possible by the remoteness of the place and the peculiar circumstances in which the ladies stood, I felt a strange weakness. The loneliness of the woods that encircled the house, and here and there afforded a distant glimpse of snow-clad peaks; the absence of any link to bind me to the old life, so that at intervals it seemed unreal; the remoteness of the great world, all tended to sap my will and weaken the purpose which had brought me to this place.

On the fourth day after my coming, however, something happened to break the spell. It chanced that I came late to dinner, and entered the room hastily and without ceremony, expecting to find Madame and her sister already seated. Instead, I found them talking in a low tone by the open door, with every mark of disorder in their appearance; while Clon and Louis stood at a little distance with downcast faces and perplexed looks.

I had tune to see all this, and then my entrance wrought a sudden change. Clon and Louis sprang to attention; Madame and her sister came to the table and sat down, and made a shallow pretence of being at their ease. But Mademoiselle's face was pale, her hand trembled; and though Madame's greater self-command enabled her to carry off the matter better, I saw that she was not herself. Once or twice she spoke harshly to Louis; she fell at other times into a brown study; and when she thought I was not watching her, her face wore a look of deep anxiety.

I wondered what all this meant; and I wondered more when, after the meal, the two walked in the garden for an hour with Clon. Mademoiselle came from this interview alone, and I was sure that she had been weeping. Madame and the dark porter stayed outside some time longer; then she, too, came in, and disappeared.

Clon did not return with her, and when I went into the garden five minutes later Louis also had vanished. Save for two women who sat sewing at an upper window, the house seemed to be deserted. Not a sound broke the afternoon stillness of room or garden, and yet I felt that more was happening in this silence than appeared on the surface. I began to grow curious--suspicious; and presently slipped out myself by way of the stables, and, skirting the wood at the back of the house, gained with a little trouble the bridge which crossed the stream and led to the village.

Turning round at this point, I could see the house, and I moved a little aside into the underwood, and stood gazing at the windows, trying to unriddle the matter. It was not likely that M. de Cocheforêt would repeat his visit so soon; and, besides, the women's emotions had been those of pure dismay and grief, unmixed with any of the satisfaction to which such a meeting, though snatched by stealth, would give rise. I discarded my first thought, therefore--that he had returned unexpectedly--and I sought for another solution.

But none was on the instant forthcoming. The windows remained obstinately blind, no figures appeared on the terrace, the garden lay deserted, and without life. My departure had not, as I half expected it would, drawn the secret into light.

I watched a while, at times cursing my own meanness; but the excitement of the moment and the quest tided me over that. Then I determined to go down into the village and see whether anything was moving there. I had been down to the inn once, and had been received half sulkily, half courteously, as a person privileged at the great house, and therefore to be accepted. It would not be thought odd if I went again; and after a moment's thought, I started down the track.

This, where it ran through the wood, was so densely shaded that the sun penetrated to it little, and in patches only. A squirrel stirred at times, sliding round a trunk, or scampering across the dry leaves. Occasionally a pig grunted and moved farther into the wood. But the place was very quiet, and I do not know how it was that I surprised Clon instead of being surprised by him.

He was walking along the path before me with his eyes on the ground-- walking so slowly, and with his lean frame so bent that I might have supposed him ill if I had not remarked the steady movement of his head from right to left, and the alert touch with which he now and again displaced a clod of earth or a cluster of leaves. By-and-bye he rose stiffly, and looked round him suspiciously; but by that time I had slipped behind a trunk, and was not to be seen; and after a brief interval he went back to his task, stooping over it more closely, if possible, than before, and applying himself with even greater care.

By that time I had made up my mind that he was tracking some one. But whom? I could not make a guess at that. I only knew that the plot was thickening, and began to feel the eagerness of the chase. Of course, if the matter had not to do with Cocheforêt, it was no affair of mine; but though it seemed unlikely that anything could bring him back so soon, he might still be at the bottom of this. And, besides, I felt a natural curiosity. When Clon at last improved his pace, and went on to the village, I took up his task. I called to mind all the wood-lore I had ever known, and scanned trodden mould and crushed leaves with eager eyes. But in vain. I could make nothing of it at all, and rose at last with an aching back and no advantage.

I did not go on to the village after that, but returned to the house, where I found Madame pacing the garden. She looked up eagerly on hearing my step; and I was mistaken if she was not disappointed--if she had not been expecting some one else. She hid the feeling bravely, however, and met me with a careless word; but she turned to the house more than once while we talked, and she seemed to be all the while on the watch, and uneasy. I was not surprised when Clon's figure presently appeared in the doorway, and she left me abruptly, and went to him. I only felt more certain than before that there was something strange on foot. What it was, and whether it had to do with M. de Cocheforêt, I could not tell. But there it was, and I grew more curious the longer I remained alone.

She came back to me presently, looking thoughtful and a trifle downcast. "That was Clon, was it not?" I said, studying her face.

"Yes," she answered. She spoke absently, and did not look at me.

"How does he talk to you?" I asked, speaking a trifle curtly.

As I intended, my tone roused her. "By signs," she said.

"Is he--is he not a little mad?" I ventured. I wanted to make her talk and forget herself.

She looked at me with sudden keenness, then dropped her eyes.

"You do not like him?" she said, a note of challenge in her voice. "I have noticed that, Monsieur."

"I think he does not like me," I replied.

"He is less trustful than we are," she answered naïvely. "It is natural that he should be. He has seen more of the world."

That silenced me for a moment, but she did not seem to notice it. "I was looking for him a little while ago, and I could not find him," I said, after a pause.

"He has been into the village," she answered.

I longed to pursue the matter farther; but though she seemed to entertain no suspicion of me, I dared not run the risk. I tried her, instead, on another tack. "Mademoiselle de Cocheforêt does not seem very well to-day?" I said.

"No?" she answered carelessly. "Well, now you speak of it, I do not think she is. She is often anxious about--my husband."

She uttered the last two words with a little hesitation, and looked at me quickly when she had spoken them. We were sitting at the moment on a stone seat which had the wall of the house for a back; and, fortunately, I was toying with the branch of a creeping plant that hung over it, so that she could not see more than the side of my face. For I knew that it altered. Over my voice, however, I had more control, and I hastened to answer,

"Yes, I suppose so," as innocently as possible.

"He is at Bosost--in Spain. You knew that, I conclude?" she said, with a certain sharpness. And she looked me in the face again very directly.

"Yes," I answered, beginning to tremble.

"I suppose you have heard, too, that he--that he sometimes crosses the border?" she continued, in a low voice, but with a certain ring of insistence in her tone. "Or, if you have not heard it, you guess it?"

I was in a quandary, and grew, in one second, hot all over. Uncertain what amount of knowledge I ought to admit, I took refuge in gallantry. "I should be surprised if he did not," I answered, with a bow, "being, as he is, so close, and having such an inducement to return, Madame."

She drew a long, shivering sigh--at the thought of his peril, I fancied, and sat back against the wall. Nor did she say any more, though I heard her sigh again. In a moment she rose. "The afternoons are growing chilly," she said; "I will go in and see how Mademoiselle is. Sometimes she does not come to supper. If she cannot descend this evening, I am afraid you must excuse me too, Monsieur."

I said what was right, and watched her go in; and, as I did so, I loathed my errand, and the mean contemptible curiosity which it had planted in my mind, more than at any former time. These women--I could find it in my heart to hate them for their frankness, for their foolish confidence, and the silly trustfulness that made them so easy a prey!

Nom de Dieu! What did the woman mean by telling me all this? To meet me in such a way, to disarm one by such methods, was to take an unfair advantage. It put a vile--ay, the vilest--aspect, on the work I had to do.

Yet it was very odd! What could M. de Cocheforêt mean by returning so soon, if M. de Cocheforêt was here? And, on the other hand, if it was not his unexpected presence that had so upset the house, what was the secret? Whom had Clon been tracking? And what was the cause of Madame's anxiety? In a few minutes I began to grow curious again; and, as the ladies did not appear at supper, I had leisure to give my brain full license, and in the course of an hour thought of a hundred keys to the mystery. But none exactly fitted the lock, or laid open the secret.

A false alarm that evening helped to puzzle me still more. I was sitting, about an hour after supper, on the same seat in the garden--I had my cloak and was smoking--when Madame came out like a ghost, and, without seeing me, flitted away through the darkness toward the stables. For a moment I hesitated, then I followed her. She went down the path and round the stables, and so far I understood; but when she had in this way gained the rear of the west wing, she took a track through the thicket to the east of the house again, and so came back to the garden. This gained, she came up the path and went in through the parlour door, and disappeared--after making a clear circuit of the house, and not once pausing or looking to right or left! I confess I was fairly baffled. I sank back on the seat I had left, and said to myself that this was the lamest of all conclusions. I was sure that she had exchanged no word with any one. I was equally sure that she had not detected my presence behind her. Why, then, had she made this strange promenade, alone, unprotected, an hour after nightfall? No dog had bayed, no one had moved, she had not once paused, or listened, like a person expecting a rencontre. I could not make it out. And I came no nearer to solving it, though I lay awake an hour beyond my usual time.

In the morning neither of the ladies descended to dinner, and I heard that Mademoiselle was not so well. After a lonely meal, therefore--I missed them more than I should have supposed--I retired to my favourite seat, and fell to meditating.

The day was fine, and the garden pleasant. Sitting there with my eyes on the old-fashioned herb-beds, with the old-fashioned scents in the air, and the dark belt of trees bounding the view on either side, I could believe that I had been out of Paris not three weeks, but three months. The quiet lapped me round. I could fancy that I had never loved anything else. The wood-doves cooed in the stillness; occasionally the harsh cry of a jay jarred the silence. It was an hour after noon, and hot. I think I nodded.

On a sudden, as if in a dream, I saw Clon's face peering at me round the angle of the parlour door. He looked, and in a moment withdrew, and I heard whispering. The door was gently closed. Then all was still again.

But I was wide awake now, and thinking hard. Clearly the people of the house wished to assure themselves that I was asleep and safely out of the way. As clearly, it was to my interest to know what was passing. Giving way to the temptation, I rose quietly, and, stooping below the level of the windows, slipped round the east end of the house, passing between it and the great yew hedge. Here I found all still, and no one stirring. So, keeping a wary eye about me, I went on round the house--reversing the route which Madame had taken the night before--until I gained the rear of the stables. Here I had scarcely paused a second to scan the ground before two persons came out of the stable-court They were Madame and the porter.

They stood a brief while outside, and looked up and down. Then Madame said something to the man, and he nodded. Leaving him standing where he was, she crossed the grass with a quick, light step, and vanished among the trees.

In a moment my mind was made up to follow; and, as Clon turned at once and went in, I was able to do so before it was too late. Bending low among the shrubs, I ran hot-foot to the point where Madame had entered the wood. Here I found a narrow path, and ran nimbly along it, and presently saw her grey robe fluttering among the trees before me. It only remained to keep out of her sight and give her no chance of discovering that she was followed; and this I set myself to do. Once or twice she glanced round, but the wood was of beech, the light which passed between the leaves was mere twilight, and my clothes were dark-coloured. I had every advantage, therefore, and little to fear as long as I could keep her in view and still remain myself at such a distance that the rustle of my tread would not disturb her.

Assured that she was on her way to meet her husband, whom my presence kept from the house, I felt that the crisis had come at last; and I grew more excited with each step I took. True, I detested the task of watching her: it filled me with peevish disgust. But in proportion as I hated it I was eager to have it done and be done with it, and succeed, and stuff my ears and begone from the scene. When she presently came to the verge of the beech wood, and, entering a little open clearing, seemed to loiter, I went cautiously. This, I thought, must be the rendezvous; and I held back warily, looking to see him step out of the thicket.

But he did not, and by-and-bye she quickened her pace. She crossed the open and entered a wide ride cut through a low, dense wood of alder and dwarf oak--a wood so closely planted, and so intertwined with hazel and elder and box that the branches rose like a solid wall, twelve feet high, on either side of the track.

Down this she passed, and I stood and watched her go; for I dared not follow. The ride stretched away as straight as a line for four or five hundred yards, a green path between green walls. To enter it was to be immediately detected, if she turned; while the thicket itself permitted no passage. I stood baffled and raging, and watched her pass along. It seemed an age before she at last reached the end, and, turning sharply to the right, was in an instant gone from sight.

I waited then no longer. I started off, and, running as lightly and quietly as I could, I sped down the green alley. The sun shone into it, the trees kept off the wind, and between heat and haste, I sweated finely. But the turf was soft, and the ground fell slightly, and in little more than a minute I gained the end. Fifty yards short of the turning I stayed myself, and, stealing on, looked cautiously the way she had gone.

I saw before me a second ride, the twin of the other, and a hundred and fifty paces down it her grey figure tripping on between the green hedges. I stood and took breath, and cursed the wood and the heat and Madame's wariness. We must have come a league or two-thirds of a league, at least. How far did the man expect her to plod to meet him? I began to grow angry. There is moderation even in the cooking of eggs, and this wood might stretch into Spain, for all I knew!

Presently she turned the corner and was gone again, and I had to repeat my manœuvre. This time, surely, I should find a change. But no! Another green ride stretched away into the depths of the forest, with hedges of varying shades--here light and there dark, as hazel and elder, or thorn, and yew and box prevailed--but always high and stiff and impervious. Half-way down the ride Madame's figure tripped steadily on, the only moving thing in sight. I wondered, stood, and, when she vanished, followed--only to find that she had entered another track, a little narrower, but in every other respect alike.

And so it went on for quite half an hour. Sometimes Madame turned to the right, sometimes to the left. The maze seemed to be endless. Once or twice I wondered whether she had lost her way, and was merely seeking to return. But her steady, purposeful gait, her measured pace, forbade the idea. I noticed, too, that she seldom looked behind her--rarely to right or left. Once the ride down which she passed was carpeted not with green, but with the silvery, sheeny leaves of some creeping plant that in the distance had a shimmer like that of water at evening. As she trod this, with her face to the low sun, her tall grey figure had a pure air that for the moment startled me--she looked unearthly. Then I swore in scorn of myself, and at the next corner I had my reward. She was no longer walking on. She had stopped, I found, and seated herself on a fallen tree that lay in the ride.

For some time I stood in ambush watching her, and with each minute I grew more impatient. At last I began to doubt--to have strange thoughts. The green walls were growing dark. The sun was sinking; a sharp, white peak, miles and miles away, which closed the vista of the ride began to flush and colour rosily. Finally, but not before I had had leisure to grow uneasy, she stood up and walked on more slowly. I waited, as usual, until the next turning hid her. Then I hastened after her, and, warily passing round the corner--came face to face with her!

I knew all in a moment--that she had fooled me, tricked me, lured me away. Her face was white with scorn, her eyes blazed; her figure, as she confronted me, trembled with anger and infinite contempt.

"You spy!" she cried. "You hound! You--gentleman! Oh, mon Dieu! if you are one of us--if you are really not canaille--we shall pay for this some day! We shall pay a heavy reckoning in the time to come! I did not think," she continued--her every syllable like the lash of a whip--"that there was anything so vile as you in this world!"

I stammered something--I do not know what. Her words burned into me--into my heart! Had she been a man, I would have struck her dead!

"You thought you deceived me yesterday," she continued, lowering her tone, but with no lessening of the passion and contempt which curled her lip and gave fulness to her voice. "You plotter! You surface trickster! You thought it an easy task to delude a woman--you find yourself deluded. God give you shame that you may suffer!" she continued mercilessly. "You talked of Clon, but Clon beside you is the most honourable of men!"

"Madame," I said hoarsely--and I know my face was grey as ashes--"let us understand one another."

"God forbid!" she cried, on the instant. "I would not soil myself!"

"Fie! Madame," I said, trembling. "But then, you are a woman. That should cost a man his life!"

She laughed bitterly.

"You say well," she retorted. "I am not a man. Neither am I Madame. Madame de Cocheforêt has spent this afternoon--thanks to your absence and your imbecility--with her husband. Yes, I hope that hurts you!" she went on, savagely snapping her little white teeth together. "To spy and do vile work, and do it ill, Monsieur Mouchard--Monsieur de Mouchard, I should say--I congratulate you!"

"You are not Madame de Cocheforêt!" I cried, stunned--even in the midst of my shame and rage--by this blow.

"No, Monsieur!" she answered grimly. "I am not! And permit me to point out--for we do not all lie easily--that I never said I was. You deceived yourself so skilfully that we had no need to trick you."

"Mademoiselle, then?" I muttered.

"Is Madame!" she cried. "Yes, and I am Mademoiselle de Cocheforêt. And in that character, and in all others, I beg from this moment to close our acquaintance, Sir. When we meet again--if we ever do meet--which God forbid!" she cried, her eyes sparkling, "do not presume to speak to me, or I will have you flogged by the grooms. And do not stain our roof by sleeping under it again. You may lie to-night in the inn. It shall not be said that Cocheforêt," she continued proudly, "returned even treachery with inhospitality; and I will give orders to that end. To-morrow begone back to your master, like the whipped cur you are! Spy and coward!"

With the last fierce words she moved away. I would have said something, I could almost have found it in my heart to stop her and make her hear. Nay, I had dreadful thoughts; for I was the stronger, and I might have done with her as I pleased. But she swept by me so fearlessly--as I might pass some loathsome cripple in the road--that I stood turned to stone. Without looking at me--without turning her head to see whether I followed or remained, or what I did--she went steadily down the track until the trees and the shadow and the growing darkness hid her grey figure from me; and I found myself alone.

REVENGE

And full of black rage! Had she only reproached me, or, turning on me in the hour of my victory, said all she had now said in the moment of her own, I could have borne it. She might have shamed me then, and I might have taken the shame to myself, and forgiven her. But, as it was, I stood there in the gathering dusk, between the darkening hedges, baffled, tricked, defeated! And by a woman! She had pitted her wits against mine, her woman's will against my experience, and she had come off the victor. And then she had reviled me. As I took it all in, and began to comprehend, also, the more remote results, and how completely her move had made further progress on my part impossible, I hated her. She had tricked me with her gracious ways and her slow-coming smile. And, after all--for what she had said--it was this man's life or mine. What had I done that another man would not do? Mon Dieu! In the future there was nothing I would not do. I would make her smart for those words of hers! I would bring her to her knees!

Still, hot as I was, an hour might have restored me to coolness. But when I started to return, I fell into a fresh rage, for I remembered that I did not know my way out of the maze of rides and paths into which she had drawn me; and this and the mishaps which followed kept my rage hot. For a full hour I wandered in the wood, unable, though I knew where the village lay, to find any track which led continuously in one direction. Whenever, at the end of each attempt, the thicket brought me up short, I fancied I heard her laughing on the farther side of the brake; and the ignominy of this chance punishment, the check which the confinement placed on my rage, almost maddened me. In the darkness, I fell, and rose cursing; I tore my hands with thorns; I stained my suit, which had suffered sadly once before. At length, when I had almost resigned myself to lie in the wood, I caught sight of the lights of the village, and trembling between haste and anger, pressed towards them. In a few minutes I stood in the little street.

The lights of the inn shone only fifty yards away; but before I could show myself even there pride suggested that I should do something to repair my clothes. I stopped, and scraped and brushed them; and, at the same time, did what I could to compose my features. Then I advanced to the door and knocked. Almost on the instant the landlord's voice cried from the inside, "Enter, Monsieur!"

I raised the latch and went in. The man was alone, squatting over the fire, warming his hands A black pot simmered on the ashes: as I entered, he raised the lid and peeped inside. Then he glanced over his shoulder.

"You expected me?" I said defiantly, walking to the hearth, and setting one of my damp boots on the logs.

"Yes," he answered, nodding curtly. "Your supper is just ready. I thought you would be in about this time."

He grinned as he spoke, and it was with difficulty I suppressed my wrath "Mademoiselle de Cocheforêt told you," I said, affecting indifference, "where I was?"

"Ay, Mademoiselle--or Madame," he replied, grinning afresh.

So she had told him where she had left me, and how she had tricked me! She had made me the village laughing-stock! My rage flashed out afresh at the thought, and, at the sight of his mocking face, I raised my fist.

But he read the threat in my eyes, and was up in a moment, snarling, with his hand on his knife. "Not again, Monsieur!" he cried, in his vile patois, "My head is sore still. Raise your hand, and I will rip you up as I would a pig!"

"Sit down, fool," I said. "I am not going to harm you. Where is your wife?"

"About her business."

"Which should be getting my supper," I retorted sharply.

He rose sullenly, and, fetching a platter, poured the mess of broth and vegetables into it. Then he went to a cupboard and brought out a loaf of black bread and a measure of wine, and set them also on the table. "You see it," he said laconically.

"And a poor welcome!" I exclaimed.

He flamed into sudden passion at that. Leaning with both his hands on the table, he thrust his rugged face and blood-shot eyes close to mine. His mustachios bristled; his beard trembled. "Hark ye, Sirrah!" he muttered, with sullen emphasis--"be content! I have my suspicions. And if it were not for my lady's orders I would put a knife into you, fair or foul, this very night. You would lie snug outside, instead of inside, and I do not think any one would be the worse. But, as it is, be content. Keep a still tongue; and when you turn your back on Cocheforêt to-morrow keep it turned."

"Tut! tut!" I said--but I confess I was a little out of countenance. "Threatened men live long, you rascal!"

"In Paris!" he answered significantly. "Not here, Monsieur."

He straightened himself with that, nodded once, and went back to the fire, and I shrugged my shoulders and began to eat, affecting to forget his presence. The logs on the hearth burned sullenly, and gave no light. The poor oil-lump, casting weird shadows from wall to wall, served only to discover the darkness. The room, with its low roof and earthen floor, and foul clothes flung here and there, reeked of stale meals and garlic and vile cooking. I thought of the parlour at Cocheforêt, and the dainty table, and the stillness, and the scented pot-herbs; and, though I was too old a soldier to eat the worse because my spoon lacked washing, I felt the change, and laid it savagely at Mademoiselle's door.

The landlord, watching me stealthily from his place by the hearth, read my thoughts, and chuckled aloud. "Palace fare, palace manners!" he muttered scornfully. "Set a beggar on horseback, and he will ride--back to the inn!"

"Keep a civil tongue, will you!" I answered, scowling at him.

"Have you finished?" he retorted.

I rose, without deigning to reply, and, going to the fire, drew off my boots, which were wet through. He, on the instant, swept off the wine and loaf to the cupboard, and then, coming back for the platter I had used, took it, opened the back door, and went out, leaving the door ajar. The draught which came in beat the flame of the lamp this way and that, and gave the dingy, gloomy room an air still more miserable. I rose angrily from the fire, and went to the door, intending to close it with a bang.

But when I reached it, I saw something, between door and jamb, which stayed my hand. The door led to a shed in which the housewife washed pots and the like. I felt some surprise, therefore, when I found a light there at this time of night; still more surprise when I saw what she was doing.

She was seated on the mud floor, with a rushlight before her, and on either side of her a high-piled heap of refuse and rubbish. From one of these, at the moment I caught sight of her, she was sorting things--horrible, filthy sweepings of road or floor--to the other; shaking and sifting each article as she passed it across, and then taking up another and repeating the action with it, and so on: all minutely, warily, with an air of so much patience and persistence that I stood wondering. Some things--rags--she held up between her eyes and the light, some she passed through her fingers, some she fairly tore in pieces. And all the time her husband stood watching her greedily, my platter still in his hand, as if her strange occupation fascinated him.

I stood looking, also, for half a minute, perhaps; then the man's eye, raised for a single second to the doorway, met mine. He started, muttered something to his wife, and, quick as thought, kicked the light out, leaving the shed in darkness. Cursing him for an ill-conditioned fellow, I walked back to the fire, laughing. In a twinkling he followed me, his face dark with rage.

"Ventre saint gris!" he exclaimed, thrusting it close to mine. "Is not a man's house his own?"

"It is, for me," I answered coolly, shrugging my shoulders. "And his wife: if she likes to pick dirty rags at this hour, that is your affair."

"Pig of a spy!" he cried, foaming with rage.

I was angry enough at bottom, but I had nothing to gain by quarrelling with the fellow; and I curtly bade him remember himself. "Your mistress gave you your orders," I said contemptuously. "Obey them!"

He spat on the floor, but at the same time he grew calmer. "You are right there," he answered spitefully. "What matter, after all, since you leave to-morrow at six? Your horse has been sent down, and your baggage is above."

"I will go to it," I retorted. "I want none of your company. Give me a light, fellow!"

He obeyed reluctantly, and, glad to turn my back on him, I went up the ladder, still wondering faintly, in the midst of my annoyance, what his wife was about that my chance detection of her had so enraged him. Even now he was not quite himself. He followed me with abuse, and, deprived by my departure of any other means of showing his spite, fell to shouting through the floor, bidding me remember six o'clock, and be stirring; with other taunts, which did not cease until he had tired himself out.

The sight of my belongings--which I had left a few hours before at the Château--strewn about the floor of this garret, went some way towards firing me again. But I was worn out. The indignities and mishaps of the evening had, for once, crushed my spirit, and after swearing an oath or two I began to pack my bags. Vengeance I would have; but the time and manner I left for daylight thought. Beyond six o'clock in the morning I did not look forward; and if I longed for anything it was for a little of the good Armagnac I had wasted on those louts of merchants in the kitchen below. It might have done me good now.

I had wearily strapped up one bag, and nearly filled the other, when I came upon something which did, for the moment, rouse the devil in me. This was the tiny orange-coloured sachet which Mademoiselle had dropped the night I first saw her at the inn, and which, it will be remembered, I picked up. Since that night I had not seen it, and had as good as forgotten it. Now, as I folded up my other doublet, the one I had then been wearing, it dropped from the pocket.

The sight of it recalled all--that night, and Mademoiselle's face in the lanthorn light, and my fine plans, and the end of them; and, in a fit of childish fury, the outcome of long suppressed passion, I snatched up the sachet from the floor and tore it across and across, and flung the pieces down. As they fell, a cloud of fine pungent dust burst from them, and with the dust something heavier, which tinkled sharply on the boards. I looked down to see what this was--perhaps I already repented of my act--but for the moment I could see nothing. The floor was grimy and uninviting, and the light bad.

In certain moods, however, a man is obstinate about small things, and I moved the taper nearer. As I did so, a point of light, a flashing sparkle that shone for a second among the dirt and refuse on the floor, caught my eye. It was gone in a moment, but I had seen it. I stared, and moved the light again, and the spark flashed out afresh, this time in a different place. Much puzzled, I knelt, and, in a twinkling, found a tiny crystal. Hard by lay another--and another; each as large as a fair-sized pea. I took up the three, and rose to my feet again, the light in one hand, the crystals in the palm of the other.

They were diamonds!--diamonds of price! I knew it in a moment. As I moved the taper to and fro above them, and watched the fire glow and tremble in their depths, I knew that I held that which would buy the crazy inn and all its contents a dozen times over. They were diamonds! Gems so fine, and of so rare a water--or I had never seen gems--that my hand trembled as I held them, and my head grew hot, and my heart beat furiously. For a moment I thought I dreamed, that my fancy played me some trick; and I closed my eyes and did not open them again for a minute. But when I did, there they were, hard, real, and angular. Convinced at last, in a maze of joy and fear, I closed my hand upon them, and, stealing on tip-toe to the trapdoor, laid first my saddle on it, and then my bags, and over all my cloak, breathing fast the while.

Then I stole back; and, taking up the light again, began to search the floor, patiently, inch by inch, with naked feet, every sound making me tremble as I crept hither and thither over the creaking boards. And never was search more successful or better paid. In the fragments of the sachet I found six smaller diamonds and a pair of rubies. Eight large diamonds I found on the floor. One, the largest and last-found, had bounded away, and lay against the wall in the farthest corner. It took me an hour to run that one to earth; but afterwards I spent another hour on my hands and knees before I gave up the search, and, satisfied at last that I had collected all, sat down on my saddle on the trap-door, and, by the last flickering light of a candle which I had taken from my bag, gloated over my treasure--a treasure worthy of fabled Golconda.

Hardly could I believe in its reality, even now. Recalling the jewels which the English Duke of Buckingham wore on the occasion of his visit to Paris in 1625, and of which there was so much talk, I took these to be as fine, though less in number. They should be worth fifteen thousand crowns, more or less. Fifteen thousand crowns! And I held them in the hollow of my hand--I who was scarcely worth ten thousand sous.

The candle going out cut short my admiration. Left in the dark with these precious atoms, my first thought was how I might dispose of them safely; which I did, for the time, by secreting them in the lining of my boot. My second thought turned on the question how they had come where I had found them, among the powdered spice and perfumes in Mademoiselle de Cocheforêt's sachet.

A minute's reflection enabled me to come very near the secret, and at the same time shed a flood of light on several dark places. What Clon had been seeking on the path between the house and the village, what the goodwife of the inn had sought among the sweepings of yard and floor, I knew now,--the sachet. I knew, too, what had caused the marked and sudden anxiety I had noticed at the Château--the loss of this sachet.

And there for a while I came to a check. But one step more up the ladder of thought brought all in view. In a flash I guessed how the jewels had come to be in the sachet; and that it was not Mademoiselle but M. de Cocheforêt who had mislaid them. And I thought the discovery so important that I began to pace the room softly, unable, in my excitement, to remain still.

Doubtless he had dropped the jewels in the hurry of his start from the inn that night! Doubtless, too, he had carried them in that bizarre hiding-place for the sake of safety, considering it unlikely that robbers, if he fell into their hands, would take the sachet from him; as still less likely that they would suspect it to contain anything of value. Everywhere it would pass for a love-gift, the work of his mistress.

Nor did my penetration stop there. Ten to one the gems were family property, the last treasure of the house; and M. de Cocheforêt, when I saw him at the inn, was on his way to convey them out of the country; either to secure them from seizure by the Government, or to raise money by selling them--money to be spent in some last desperate enterprise. For a day or two, perhaps, after leaving Cocheforêt, while the mountain road and its chances occupied his thoughts, he had not discovered his loss. Then he had searched for the precious sachet, missed it, and returned hot-foot on his tracks.

I was certain that I had hit on the true solution; and all that night I sat wakeful in the darkness, pondering what I should do. The stones, unset as they were, could never be identified, never be claimed. The channel by which they had come to my hands could never be traced. To all intents they were mine--mine, to do with as I pleased! Fifteen thousand crowns!-- perhaps twenty thousand crowns!--and I to leave at six in the morning, whether I would or no! I might leave for Spain with the jewels in my pocket.

I confess I was tempted. The gems were so fine that I doubt not some indifferently honest men would have sold salvation for them. But a Berault his honour? No! I was tempted, but not for long. Thank God, a man may be reduced to living by the fortunes of the dice, and may even be called by a woman spy and coward without becoming a thief. The temptation soon left me--I take credit for it--and I fell to thinking of this and that plan for making use of them. Once it occurred to me to take the jewels to the Cardinal and buy my pardon with them; again, to use them as a trap to capture Cocheforêt; again to--and then about five in the morning, as I sat up on my wretched pallet, while the first light stole slowly in through the cobwebbed, hay-stuffed lattice, there came to me the real plan, the plan of plans, on which I acted.

It charmed me. I smacked my lips over it, and hugged myself, and felt my eyes dilate in the darkness, as I conned it. It seemed cruel, it seemed mean; I cared nothing. Mademoiselle had boasted of her victory over me, of her woman's wits and her acuteness; and of my dulness. She had said her grooms should flog me, she had rated me as if I had been a dog. Very well; we would see now whose brains were the better, whose was the master mind, whose should be the whipping.

The one thing required by my plan was that I should get speech with her; that done, I could trust myself, and my new-found weapon, for the rest. But that was absolutely necessary; and seeing that there might be some difficulty about it, I determined to descend as if my mind were made up to go; then, on pretence of saddling my horse, I would slip away on foot, and lie in wait near the Château until I saw her come out. Or if I could not effect my purpose in that way--either by reason of the landlord's vigilance, or for any other cause--my course was still easy. I would ride away, and when I had proceeded a mile or so, tie up my horse in the forest and return to the wooden bridge. Thence I could watch the garden and front of the Château until time and chance gave me the opportunity I sought.

So I saw my way quite clearly; and when the fellow below called me, reminding me rudely that I must be going, and that it was six o'clock, I was ready with my answer. I shouted sulkily that I was coming, and, after a decent delay, I took up my saddle and bags and went down.

Viewed by the cold morning light, the inn room looked more smoky, more grimy, more wretched than when I had last seen it. The goodwife was not visible. The fire was not lighted. No provision, not so much as a stirrup-cup or bowl of porridge cheered the heart. I looked round, sniffing the stale smell of last night's lamp, and grunted. "Are you going to send me out fasting?" I said, affecting a worse humour than I felt.

The landlord was standing by the window, stooping over a great pair of frayed and furrowed thigh-boots, which he was labouring to soften with copious grease. "Mademoiselle ordered no breakfast," he answered, with a malicious grin.

"Well, it does not much matter," I replied grandly. "I shall be at Auch by noon."

"That is as may be," he answered, with another grin. I did not understand him, but I had something else to think about, and I opened the door and stepped out, intending to go to the stable. Then in a second I comprehended. The cold air laden with woodland moisture met me and went to my bones; but it was not that which made me shiver. Outside the door, in the road, sitting on horseback in silence, were two men. One was Clon. The other, who held a spare horse by the rein--my horse--was a man I had seen at the inn, a rough, shock-headed, hard-bitten fellow. Both were armed, and Clon was booted. His mate rode barefoot, with a rusty spur strapped to one heel.

The moment I saw them a sure and certain fear crept into my mind: it was that made me shiver. But I did not speak to them. I went in again, and closed the door behind me. The landlord was putting on the boots. "What does this mean?" I said hoarsely. I had a clear prescience of what was coming. "Why are these men here?"

"Orders," he answered laconically.

"Whose orders?" I retorted.

"Whose?" he answered bluntly. "Well, Monsieur, that is my business. Enough that we mean to see you out of the country, and out of harm's way."

"But if I will not go?" I cried.

"Monsieur will go," he answered coolly. "There are no strangers in the village to-day," he added, with a significant smile.

"Do you mean to kidnap me?" I replied, in a rage. Behind the rage was something--I will not call it terror, for the brave feel no terror--but it was near akin to it. I had had to do with rough men all my life, but there was a grimness and truculence in the aspect of these three that shook me. When I thought of the dark paths and narrow lanes and cliff-sides we must traverse, whichever road we took, I trembled.

"Kidnap you, Monsieur?" he answered, with an everyday air. "That is as you please to call it. One thing is certain, however," he continued, maliciously touching an arquebuss which he had produced and set upright against a chair while I was at the door; "if you attempt the slightest resistance, we shall know how to put an end to it, either here or on the road."

I drew a deep breath. The very imminence of the danger restored me to the use of my faculties I changed my tone and laughed aloud. "So that is your plan, is it?" I said. "The sooner we start the better, then. And the sooner I see Auch and your back turned, the more I shall be pleased."

He rose. "After you, Monsieur," he said.

I could not restrain a slight shiver. His newborn politeness alarmed me more than his threats. I knew the man and his ways, and I was sure that it boded ill for me.

But I had no pistols, and only my sword and knife, and I knew that resistance at this point must be worse than vain. I went out jauntily, therefore, the landlord coming after me with my saddle and bags.

The street was empty, save for the two waiting horsemen who sat in their saddles looking doggedly before them. The sun had not yet risen, the air was raw. The sky was grey, cloudy, and cold. My thoughts flew back to the morning on which I had found the sachet--at that very spot, almost at that very hour; and for a moment I grew warm again at the thought of the little packet I carried in my boot. But the landlord's dry manner, the sullen silence of his two companions, whose eyes steadily refused to meet mine, chilled me again. For an instant the impulse to refuse to mount, to refuse to go, was almost irresistible; then, knowing the madness of such a course, which might, and probably would, give the men the chance they desired, I crushed it down and went slowly to my stirrup.

"I wonder you do not want my sword," I said by way of sarcasm, as I swung myself up.

"We are not afraid of it," the innkeeper answered gravely. "You may keep it--for the present."

I made no answer--what answer had I to make?--and we rode at a foot-pace down the street; he and I leading, Clon and the shock-headed man bringing up the rear. The leisurely mode of our departure, the absence of hurry or even haste, the men's indifference whether they were seen, or what was thought, all served to sink my spirits, and deepen my sense of peril. I felt that they suspected me, that they more than half guessed the nature of my errand at Cocheforêt, and that they were not minded to be bound by Mademoiselle's orders. In particular I augured the worst from Clon's appearance. His lean malevolent face and sunken eyes, his very dumbness chilled me. Mercy had no place there.

We rode soberly, so that nearly half an hour elapsed before we gained the brow from which I had taken my first look at Cocheforêt. Among the dwarf oaks whence I had viewed the valley we paused to breathe our horses, and the strange feelings with which I looked back on the scene may be imagined. But I had short time for indulging in sentiment or recollections. A curt word, and we were moving again.

A quarter of a mile farther on the road to Auch dipped into the valley. When we were already half-way down this descent the innkeeper suddenly stretched out his hand and caught my rein. "This way!" he said.

I saw he would have me turn into a by-path leading south-westwards--a mere track, faint and little trodden and encroached on by trees, which led I knew not whither. I checked my horse. "Why?" I said rebelliously. "Do you think I do not know the road? This is the way to Auch."

"To Auch--yes," he answered bluntly. "But we are not going to Auch."

"Whither then?" I said angrily.

"You will see presently," he replied, with an ugly smile.

"Yes, but I will know now!" I retorted, passion getting the better of me. "I have come so far with you. You will find it more easy to take me farther, if you tell me your plans."

"You are a fool!" he cried, with a snarl.

"Not so," I answered. "I ask only to know whither I am going."

"Into Spain," he said. "Will that satisfy you?"

"And what will you do with me there?" I asked, my heart giving a great bound.

"Hand you over to some friends of ours," he answered curtly, "if you behave yourself. If not, there is a shorter way, and one that will save us some travelling. Make up your mind. Monsieur. Which shall it be?"

UNDER THE PIC DU MIDI

So that was their plan. Two or three hours to the southward, the long white glittering wall stretched east and west above the brown woods. Beyond that lay Spain. Once across the border, I might be detained, if no worse happened to me, as a prisoner of war; for we were then at war with Spain on the Italian side. Or I might be handed over to one of the savage bands, half smugglers, half brigands, that held the passes; or be delivered--worst fate of all--into the power of the French exiles, of whom some would be likely to recognize me and cut my throat.

"It is a long way into Spain," I muttered, watching in a kind of fascination Clon handling his pistols.

"I think you will find the other road longer still!" the landlord answered grimly. "But choose, and be quick about it."

They were three to one, and they had firearms. In effect I had no choice. "Well, if I must I must!" I cried, making up my mind with seeming recklessness. "Vogue la galère! Spain be it. It will not be the first time I have heard the dons talk."

The men nodded, as much as to say that they had known what the end would be; the landlord released my rein; and in a trice we were riding down the narrow track, with our faces set towards the mountains.

On one point my mind was now more easy. The men meant fairly by me; and I had no longer to fear, as I had feared, a pistol shot in the back at the first convenient ravine. As far as that went, I might ride in peace. On the other hand, if I let them carry me across the border my fate was sealed. A man set down without credentials or guards among the wild desperadoes who swarmed in war time in the Asturian passes might consider himself fortunate if an easy death fell to his lot. In my case I could make a shrewd guess what would happen. A single nod of meaning, one muttered word, dropped among the savage men with whom I should be left, and the diamonds hidden in my boot would go neither to the Cardinal nor back to Mademoiselle--nor would it matter to me whither they went.

So while the others talked in their taciturn fashion, or sometimes grinned at my gloomy face, I looked out over the brown woods with eyes that saw, yet did not see. The red squirrel swarming up the trunk, the startled pigs that rushed away grunting from their feast of mast, the solitary rider who met us, armed to the teeth, and passed northwards after whispering with the landlord--all these I saw. But my mind was not with them. It was groping and feeling about like a hunted mole for some way of escape. For time pressed. The slope we were on was growing steeper. By-and-bye we fell into a southward valley, and began to follow it steadily upwards, crossing and recrossing a swiftly rushing stream. The snow-peaks began to be hidden behind the rising bulk of hills that overhung us; and sometimes we could see nothing before or behind but the wooded walls of our valley rising sheer and green a thousand paces on either hand, with grey rocks half masked by fern and ivy getting here and there through the firs and alders.

It was a wild and sombre scene even at that hour, with the midday sun shining on the rushing water and drawing the scent out of the pines; but I knew that there was worse to come, and sought desperately for some ruse by which I might at least separate the men. Three were too many; with one I might deal. At last, when I had cudgelled my brain for an hour, and almost resigned myself to a sudden charge on the men single-handed--a last desperate resort--I thought of a plan, dangerous, too, and almost desperate, but which still seemed to promise something. It came of my fingers resting in my pocket on the fragments of the orange sachet, which, without having any particular design in my mind, I had taken care to bring with me. I had torn the sachet into four pieces--four corners. As I played mechanically with them, one of my fingers fitted into one, as into a glove; a second finger into another. And the plan came.

Still, before I could move in it, I had to wait until we stopped to bait the flagging horses, which we did about noon at the head of the valley. Then, pretending to drink from the stream, I managed to secure unseen a handful of pebbles, slipping them into the same pocket with the morsels of stuff. On getting to horse again, I carefully fitted a pebble, not too tightly, into the largest scrap, and made ready for the attempt.

The landlord rode on my left, abreast of me; the other two knaves behind. The road at this stage favoured me, for the valley, which drained the bare uplands that lay between the lower spurs and the base of the real mountains, had become wide and shallow. Here were no trees, and the path was a mere sheep-track covered with short crisp grass, and running sometimes on this bank of the stream and sometimes on that.

I waited until the ruffian beside me turned to speak to the men behind.

The moment he did so and his eyes were averted, I slipped out the scrap of satin in which I had placed the pebble, and balancing it carefully on my right thigh as I rode, I flipped it forward with all the strength of my thumb and finger. I meant it to fall a few paces before us in the path, where it could be seen. But alas for my hopes! At the critical moment my horse started, my finger struck the scrap aslant, the pebble flew out, and the bit of stuff fluttered into a whin-bush close to my stirrup--and was lost!

I was bitterly disappointed, for the same thing might happen again, and I had now only three scraps left. But fortune favoured me, by putting it into my neighbour's head to plunge into a hot debate with the shock-headed man on the nature of some animals seen on a distant brow; which he said were izards, while the other maintained that they were common goats. He continued, on this account, to ride with his face turned the other way. I had time to fit another pebble into the second piece of stuff, and sliding it on to my thigh, poised it, and flipped it.

This time my finger struck the tiny missile fairly in the middle, and shot it so far and so truly that it dropped exactly in the path ten paces in front of us. The moment I saw it fall I kicked my neighbour's nag in the ribs; it started, and he, turning in a rage, hit it. The next instant he pulled it almost on to its haunches.

"Saint Gris!" he cried; and sat glaring at the bit of yellow satin, with his face turned purple and his jaw fallen.

"What is it?" I said, staring at him in turn. "What is the matter, fool?"

"Matter?" he blurted out. "Mon Dieu!"

But Clon's excitement surpassed even his. The dumb man no sooner saw what had attracted his comrade's attention, than he uttered an inarticulate and horrible noise, and tumbling off his horse, more like a beast than a man, threw himself bodily on the precious morsel.

The innkeeper was not far behind him. An instant and he was down, too, peering at the thing; and for an instant I thought that they would fight over it. However, though their jealousy was evident, their excitement cooled a little when they discovered that the scrap of stuff was empty; for, fortunately, the pebble had fallen out of it. Still, it threw them into such a fever of eagerness as it was wonderful to witness. They nosed the ground where it had lain, they plucked up the grass and turf, and passed it through their fingers, they ran to and fro like dogs on a trail; and, glancing askance at one another, came back always together to the point of departure. Neither in his jealousy would suffer the other to be there alone.

The shock-headed man and I sat our horses and looked on; he marvelling, and I pretending to marvel. As the two searched up and down the path, we moved a little out of it to give them space; and presently, when all their heads were turned from me, I let a second morsel drop under a gorse-bush. The shock-headed man, by-and-bye, found this, and gave it to

Clon; and, as from the circumstances of the first discovery no suspicion attached to me, I ventured to find the third and last scrap myself. I did not pick it up, but I called the innkeeper, and he pounced on it as I have seen a hawk pounce on a chicken.

They hunted for the fourth morsel, but, of course, in vain, and in the end they desisted, and fitted the three they had together; but neither would let his own portion out of his hands, and each looked at the other across the spoil with eyes of suspicion. It was strange to see them in that wide-stretching valley, whence grey boar-backs of hills swelled up into the silence of the snow--it was strange, I say, in that vast solitude to see these two, mere dots on its bosom, circling round one another in fierce forgetfulness of the outside world, glaring and shifting their ground like cocks about to engage, and wholly engrossed--by three scraps of orange-colour, invisible at fifty paces!

At last the innkeeper cried with an oath: "I am going back. This must be known down yonder. Give me your pieces, man, and do you go with Antoine. It will be all right."

But Clon, waving a scrap in either hand and thrusting his ghastly mask into the other's face, shook his head in passionate denial. He could not speak, but he made it clear that if any one went back with the news he was the man to go.

"Nonsense!" the landlord retorted fiercely. "We cannot leave Antoine to go on alone with him. Give me the stuff."

But Clon would not. He had no thought of resigning the credit of the discovery, and I began to think that the two would really come to blows. But there was an alternative, and first one and then the other looked at me. It was a moment of peril, and I knew it. My stratagem might react on myself, and the two, to put an end to this difficulty, agree to put an end to me. But I faced them so coolly and showed so bold a front, and the ground was so open, that the idea took no root. They fell to wrangling again more viciously than before. One tapped his gun and the other his pistols. The landlord scolded, the dumb man gurgled. At last their difference ended as I had hoped it would.

"Very well then, we will both go back!" the innkeeper cried in a rage. "And Antoine must see him on. But the blame be on your head. Do you give the lad your pistols."

Clon took one pistol and gave it to the shock-headed man.

"The other!" the innkeeper said impatiently.

But Clon shook his head with a grim smile, and pointed to the arquebuss.

By a sudden movement the landlord snatched the pistol, and averted Clon's vengeance by placing both it and the gun in the shock-headed man's hands. "There!" he said, addressing the latter, "now can you do? If

Monsieur tries to escape or turn back, shoot him! But four hours' riding should bring you to the Roca Blanca. You will find the men there, and will have no more to do with it."

Antoine did not see things quite in that light, however. He looked at me, and then at the wild track in front of us; and he muttered an oath and said he would die if he would. But the landlord, who was in a frenzy of impatience, drew him aside and talked to him, and in the end seemed to persuade him; for in a few minutes the matter was settled. Antoine came back and said sullenly, "Forward, Monsieur," the two others stood on one side, I shrugged my shoulders and kicked up my horse, and in a twinkling we two were riding on together--man to man. I turned once or twice to see what those we had left behind were doing, and always found them standing in apparent debate; but my guard showed so much jealousy of these movements that I presently shrugged my shoulders again and desisted.

I had racked my brains to bring about this state of things. But, strange to say, now I had succeeded, I found it less satisfactory than I had hoped. I had reduced the odds and got rid of my most dangerous antagonists; but Antoine, left to himself, proved to be as full of suspicion as an egg of meat. He rode a little behind me with his gun across his saddle-bow, and a pistol near his hand, and at the slightest pause on my part, or if I turned to look at him, he muttered his constant "Forward, Monsieur!" in a tone that warned me that his finger was on the trigger. At such a distance he could not miss; and I saw nothing for it but to go on meekly before him--to the Roca Blanca and my fate.

What was to be done? The road presently reached the end of the valley and entered a narrow pine-clad defile, strewn with rocks and boulders, over which the torrent plunged and eddied with a deafening roar. In front the white gleam of waterfalls broke the sombre ranks of climbing trunks. The snow-line lay less than half a mile away on either hand; and crowning all--at the end of the pass, as it seemed to the eye--rose the pure white pillar of the Pic du Midi shooting up six thousand feet into the blue of heaven. Such a scene, so suddenly disclosed, was enough to drive the sense of danger from my mind; and for a moment I reined in my horse. But "Forward, Monsieur!" came the grating order. I fell to earth again, and went on. What was to be done?

I was at my wit's end to know. The man refused to talk, refused to ride abreast of me, would have no dismounting, no halting, no communication; at all. He would have nothing but this silent, lonely procession of two, with the muzzle of his gun at my back. And meanwhile we were fast climbing the pass. We had left the others an hour--nearly two. The sun was declining; the time, I supposed, about half-past three.

If he would only let me come within reach of him! Or if anything would fall out to take his attention! When the pass presently widened into a bare and dreary valley, strewn with huge boulders, and with snow lying here and there in the hollows, I looked desperately before me, and scanned even the vast snow-fields that overhung us and stretched away to the base of the ice-peak. But I saw nothing. No bear swung across the path, no izard showed itself on the cliffs. The keen sharp air cut our cheeks and warned me that we were approaching the summit of the ridge. On all sides were silence and desolation.

Mon Dieu! And the ruffians on whose tender mercies I was to be thrown might come to meet us! They might appear at any moment. In my despair I loosened my hat on my head, and let the first gust carry it to the ground, and then with an oath of annoyance tossed my feet loose to go after it. But the rascal roared to me to keep my seat.

"Forward, Monsieur!" he shouted brutally. "Go on!"

"But my hat!" I cried. "Mille tonnerres, man! I must--"

"Forward, Monsieur, or I shoot!" he replied inexorably, raising his gun. "One--two--"

And I went on. But, oh, I was wrathful! That I, Gil de Berault, should be outwitted and led by the nose, like a ringed bull, by this Gascon lout! That I, whom all Paris knew and feared--if it did not love--the terror of Zaton's, should come to my end in this dismal waste of snow and rock, done to death by some pitiful smuggler or thief! It must not be! Surely in the last resort I could give an account of one man, though his belt were stuffed with pistols!

But how? Only, it seemed, by open force. My heart began to flutter as I planned it; and then grew steady again. A hundred paces before us a gully or ravine on the left ran up into the snow-field. Opposite its mouth a jumble of stones and broken rocks covered the path. I marked this for the place. The knave would need both his hands to hold up his nag over the stones, and, if I turned on him suddenly enough, he might either drop his gun, or fire it harmlessly.

But, in the meantime, something happened; as, at the last moment, things do happen. While we were still fifty yards short of the place, I found his horse's nose creeping forward on a level with my crupper; and, still advancing, until I could see it out of the tail of my eye, and my heart gave a great bound. He was coming abreast of me: he was going to deliver himself into my hands! To cover my excitement, I began to whistle.

"Hush!" he muttered fiercely: his voice sounding strange and unnatural. My first thought was that he was ill, and I turned to him. But he only said again, "Hush! Pass by here quietly, Monsieur."

"Why?" I asked mutinously, curiosity getting the better of me. For had I been wise I had taken no notice; every second his horse was coming up with mine. Its nose was level with my stirrup already.

"Hush, man!" he said again. This time there was no mistake about the panic in his voice. "They call this the Devil's Chapel. God send us safe by it! It is late to be here. Look at those!" he continued, pointing with a finger which visibly shook.

I looked. At the mouth of the gully, in a small space partly cleared of stones stood three broken shafts, raised on rude pedestals. "Well?" I said in a low voice. The sun which was near setting flushed the great peak above to the colour of blood; but the valley was growing grey and each moment more dreary. "Well, what of those?" I said. In spite of my peril and the excitement of the coming struggle I felt the chill of his fear. Never had I seen so grim, so desolate, so Godforsaken a place! Involuntarily I shivered.

"They were crosses," he muttered, in a voice little above a whisper, while his eyes roved this way and that in terror. "The Curé of Gabas blessed the place, and set them up. But next morning they were as you see them now. Come on, Monsieur, come on!" he continued, plucking at my arm. "It is not safe here after sunset. Pray God, Satan be not at home!"

He had completely forgotten in his panic that he had anything to fear from me. His gun dropped loosely across his saddle, his leg rubbed mine. I saw this, and I changed my plan of action. As our horses reached the stones I stooped, as if to encourage mine, and by a sudden clutch snatched the gun bodily from his hand; at the same time I backed my horse with all my strength. It was done in a moment! A second and I had him at the end of the gun, and my finger was on the trigger. Never was victory more easily gained.

He looked at me between rage and terror, his jaw fallen. "Are you mad?" he cried, his teeth chattering as he spoke. Even in this strait his eyes left me and wandered round in alarm.

"No, sane!" I retorted fiercely. "But I do not like this place any better than you do!" Which was true enough, if not quite true. "So, by your right, quick march!" I continued imperatively. "Turn your horse, my friend, or take the consequences."

He turned like a lamb, and headed down the valley again, without giving a thought to his pistols. I kept close to him, and in less than a minute we had left the Devil's Chapel well behind us, and were moving down again as we had come up. Only now I held the gun.

When we had gone half a mile or so--until then I did not feel comfortable myself, and though I thanked Heaven the place existed, thanked Heaven also that I was out of it--I bade him halt. "Take off your belt!" I said curtly, "and throw it down. But, mark me, if you turn, I fire!"

The spirit was quite gone out of him. He obeyed mechanically. I jumped down, still covering him with the gun, and picked up the belt, pistols and all. Then I remounted, and we went on. By-and-bye he asked me sullenly what I was going to do.

"Go back," I said, "and take the road to Auch when I come to it."

"It will be dark in an hour," he answered sulkily.

"I know that," I retorted. "We must camp and do the best we can."

And as I said, we did. The daylight held until we gained the skirts of the pine-wood at the head of the pass. Here I chose a corner a little off the track, and well-sheltered from the wind, and bade him light a fire. I tethered the horses near this and within sight. It remained only to sup. I had a piece of bread; he had another and an onion. We ate in silence, sitting on opposite sides of the fire.

But after supper I found myself in a dilemma; I did not see how I was to sleep. The ruddy light which gleamed on the knave's swart face and sinewy hands showed also his eyes, black, sullen, and watchful. I knew that the man was plotting revenge; that he would not hesitate to plant his knife between my ribs should I give him a chance. I could find only one alternative to remaining awake. Had I been bloody-minded, I should have chosen it and solved the question at once and in my favour by shooting him as he sat.

But I have never been a cruel man, and I could not find it in my heart to do this. The silence of the mountain and the sky--which seemed a thing apart from the roar of the torrent and not to be broken by it--awed me. The vastness of the solitude in which we sat, the dark void above through which the stars kept shooting, the black gulf below in which the unseen waters boiled and surged, the absence of other human company or other signs of human existence put such a face upon the deed that I gave up the thought of it with a shudder, and resigned myself, instead, to watch through the night--the long, cold, Pyrenean night. Presently he curled himself up like a dog and slept in the blaze, and then for a couple of hours I sat opposite him, thinking. It seemed years since I had seen Zaton's or thrown the dice. The old life, the old employments--should I ever go back to them?--seemed dim and distant. Would Cocheforêt, the forest and the mountain, the grey Château and its mistresses, seem one day as dim! And if one bit of life could fade so quickly at the unrolling of another, and seem in a moment pale and colourless, would all life some day and somewhere, and all the things we-- But faugh! I was growing foolish. I sprang up and kicked the wood together, and, taking up the gun, began to pace to and fro under the cliff. Strange that a little moonlight, a few stars, a breath of solitude should carry a man back to childhood and childish things!

It was three in the afternoon of the next day, and the sun lay hot on the oak groves, and the air was full of warmth as we began to climb the slope, on which the road to Auch shoots out of the track. The yellow bracken and the fallen leaves underfoot seemed to throw up light of themselves, and here and there a patch of ruddy beech lay like a bloodstain on the hillside. In front a herd of pigs routed among the mast, and grunted lazily; and high above us a boy lay watching them. "We part here," I said to my companion. It was my plan to ride a little way on the road to Auch so as to blind his eyes; then, leaving my horse in the forest, I would go on foot to the Château.

"The sooner the better!" he answered, with a snarl. "And I hope I may never see your face again, Monsieur!"

But when we came to the wooden cross at the fork of the roads, and were about to part, the boy we had seen leapt out of the fern and came to meet us. "Hollo!" he cried, in a sing-song tone.

"Well!" my companion answered, drawing rein impatiently. "What is it?"

"There are soldiers in the village."

"Soldiers?" Antoine cried incredulously.

"Ay, devils on horseback!" the lad answered, spitting on the ground. "Three score of them! From Auch!"

Antoine turned to me, his face transformed with fury. "Curse you!" he cried. "This is some of your work! Now we are all undone! And my mistresses! Sacré! if I had that gun I would shoot you like a rat!"

"Steady, fool!" I answered roughly. "I know no more of this than you do!"

This was so true that my surprise was as great as his. The Cardinal, who rarely made a change of front, had sent me hither that he might not be forced to send soldiers, and run the risk of all that might arise from such a movement. What of this invasion, then, than which nothing could be less consistent with his plans? I wondered. It was possible, of course, that the travelling merchants, before whom I had played at treason, had reported the facts; and that on this the Commandant at Auch had acted. But it seemed unlikely. He had had his orders, too; and, under the Cardinal's rule, there was small place for individual enterprise. I could not understand it.

One thing was clear, however. I might now enter the village as I pleased. "I am going on to look into this," I said to Antoine. "Come, my man."

He shrugged his shoulders, and stood still. "Not I!" he answered, with an oath. "No soldiers for me! I have lain out one night, and I can lie out another!"

I nodded indifferently, for I no longer wanted him; and we parted. After this, twenty minutes' riding brought me to the entrance of the village; and here the change was great indeed. Not one of the ordinary dwellers in the place was to be seen: either they had shut themselves up in their hovels, or, like Antoine, they had fled to the woods. Their doors were closed, their windows shuttered. But lounging about the street were a score of dragoons, in boots and breastplates, whose short-barrelled muskets, with pouches and bandoliers attached, were piled near the inn door. In an open space where there was a gap in the street, a long row of horses, linked head to head, stood bending their muzzles over bundles of rough forage, and on all sides the cheerful jingle of chains and bridles and the sound of coarse jokes and laughter filled the air.

As I rode up to the inn door an old sergeant, with squinting eyes and his tongue in his cheeks, eyed me inquisitively, and started to cross the street to challenge me. Fortunately, at that moment the two knaves whom I had brought from Paris with me, and whom I had left at Auch to await my orders, came up. I made them a sign not to speak to me, and they passed on; but I suppose that they told the sergeant that I was not the man he wanted, for I saw no more of him.

After picketing my horse behind the inn--I could find no better stable, every place being full--I pushed my way through the group at the door, and entered. The old room, with the low grimy roof and the reeking floor, was half full of strange figures, and for a few minutes I stood unseen in the smoke and confusion. Then the landlord came my way, and as he passed me I caught his eye. He uttered a low curse, dropped the pitcher he was carrying, and stood glaring at me, like a man possessed.

The soldier whose wine he was carrying flung a crust in his face, with, "Now, greasy fingers! What are you staring at?"

"The devil!" the landlord muttered, beginning to tremble.

"Then let me look at him!" the man retorted and he turned on his stool.

He started, finding me standing over him. "At your service!" I said grimly. "A little time and it will be the other way, my friend."

A MASTER STROKE

I HAVE a way with me which commonly commands respect; and when the landlord's first terror was over and he would serve me, I managed to get my supper--the first good meal I had had in two days--pretty comfortably in spite of the soldiers' presence. The crowd, too, which filled the room, soon began to melt. The men strayed off in groups to water their horses, or went to hunt up their quarters, until only two or three were left. Dusk had fallen outside; the noise in the street grew less. The firelight began to glow and flicker on the walls, and the wretched room to look as homely as it was in its nature to look. I was pondering for the twentieth time what step I should take next--under these new circumstances--and why the soldiers were here, and whether I should let the night pass before I moved, when the door, which had been turning on its hinges almost without pause for an hour, opened again, and a woman came in.

She paused a moment on the threshold looking round, and I saw that she had a shawl on her head and a milk-pitcher in her hand, and that her feet and ankles were bare. There was a great rent in her coarse stuff petticoat, and the hand which held the shawl together was brown and dirty. More I did not see; supposing her to be a neighbour stolen in now that the house was quiet to get some milk for her child or the like, I took no further heed of her. I turned to the fire again and plunged into my thoughts.

But to get to the hearth where the goodwife was fidgeting, the woman had to pass in front of me; and as she passed I suppose she stole a look at me from under her shawl. For just when she came between me and the blaze she uttered a low cry and shrank aside--so quickly that she almost stepped on the hearth. The next moment she turned her back to me and was stooping, whispering in the housewife's ear. A stranger might have thought that she had merely trodden on a hot ember.

But another idea, and a very sharp one, came into my mind; and I stood up silently. The woman's back was towards me, but something in her height, her shape, the pose of her head, hidden as it was by her shawl, seemed familiar. I waited while she hung over the fire whispering, and while the goodwife slowly filled her pitcher out of the great black pot. But when she turned to go, I took a step forward so as to bar her way. And our eyes met.

I could not see her features; they were lost in the shadow of the hood. But I saw a shiver run through her from head to foot. And I knew then that I had made no mistake.

"That is too heavy for you, my girl," I said familiarly, as I might have spoken to a village wench. "I will carry it for you."

One of the men, who remained lolling at the table, laughed, and the other began to sing a low song. The woman trembled in rage or fear, but she kept silence and let me take the jug from her hands. And when I went to the door and opened it, she followed mechanically. An instant, and the door fell to behind us, shutting off the light and glow, and we two stood together in the growing dusk.

"It is late for you to be out, Mademoiselle," I said politely. "You might meet with some rudeness, dressed as you are. Permit me to see you home."

She shuddered, and I thought I heard her sob, but she did not answer. Instead, she turned and walked quickly through the village in the direction of the Château, keeping in the shadow of the houses. I carried the pitcher and walked beside her; and in the dark I smiled. I knew how shame and impotent rage were working in her. This was something like revenge!

Presently I spoke. "Well, Mademoiselle," I said. "Where are your grooms?"

She gave me one look, her eyes blazing with anger, her face like hate itself; and after that I said no more, but left her in peace, and contented myself with walking at her shoulder until we came to the end of the village, where the track to the great house plunged into the wood. There she stopped, and turned on me like a wild creature at bay. "What do you want?" she cried hoarsely, breathing as if she had been running.

"To see you safe to the house," I answered coolly.

"And if I will not?" she retorted.

"The choice does not lie with you, Mademoiselle," I answered sternly. "You will go to the house with me, and on the way you will give me an interview; but not here. Here we are not private enough. We may be interrupted at any moment, and I wish to speak to you at length."

I saw her shiver. "What if I will not?" she said again.

"I might call to the nearest soldiers and tell them who you are," I answered coolly. "I might, but I should not. That were a clumsy way of punishing you, and I know a better way. I should go to the captain, Mademoiselle, and tell him whose horse is locked up in the inn stable. A trooper told me--as some one had told him--that it belonged to one of his officers; but I looked through the crack, and I knew the horse again."

She could not repress a groan. I waited. Still she did not speak. "Shall I go to the captain?" I said ruthlessly.

She shook the hood back from her face, and looked at me. "Oh, you coward! you coward!" she hissed through her teeth. "If I had a knife!"

"But you have not, Mademoiselle," I answered, unmoved. "Be good enough, therefore, to make up your mind which it is to be. Am I to go with my news to the captain, or am I to come with you?"

"Give me the pitcher!" she said harshly.

I did so, wondering. In a moment she flung it with a savage gesture far into the bushes. "Come!" she said, "if you will. But some day God will punish you!"

Without another word she turned and entered the path through the trees, and I followed her. I suppose every turn in its course, every hollow and broken place in it had been known to her from childhood, for she followed it swiftly and unerringly, barefoot as she was. I had to walk fast through the darkness to keep up with her. The wood was quiet, but the frogs were beginning to croak in the pool, and their persistent chorus reminded me of the night when I had come to the house-door hurt and worn out, and Clon had admitted me, and she had stood under the gallery in the hall. Things had looked dark then. I had seen but a very little way ahead. Now all was plain. The Commandant might be here with all his soldiers, but it was I who held the strings.

We came to the little wooden bridge and saw beyond the dark meadows the lights of the house. All the windows were bright. Doubtless the troopers were making merry. "Now, Mademoiselle," I said quietly. "I must trouble you to stop here, and give me your attention for a few minutes. Afterwards you may go your way."

"Speak!" she said defiantly. "And be quick! I cannot breathe the air where you are! It poisons me!"

"Ah!" I said slowly. "Do you think you make things better by such speeches as those?"

"Oh!" she cried--and I heard her teeth click together. "Would you have me fawn on you?"

"Perhaps not," I answered. "Still you make one mistake."

"What is it?" she panted.

"You forget that I am to be feared as well as--loathed!" I answered grimly. "Ay, Mademoiselle, to be feared!" I continued. "Do you think that I do not know why you are here in this guise? Do you think that I do not know for whom that pitcher of broth was intended? Or who will now have to fast to-night? I tell you I know all these things. Your house is full of soldiers; your servants were watched and could not leave. You had to come yourself and get food for him!"

She clutched at the hand-rail of the bridge, and for an instant clung to it for support. Her face, from which the shawl had fallen, glimmered white in the shadow of the trees. At last I had shaken her pride. At last! "What is your price?" she murmured faintly.

"I am going to tell you," I replied, speaking so that every word might fall distinctly on her ears, and sating my eyes on her proud face. I had never dreamed of such revenge as this! "About a fortnight ago, M. de Cocheforêt left here at night with a little orange-coloured sachet in his possession."

She uttered a stifled cry, and drew herself stiffly erect.

"It contained--but there, Mademoiselle, you know its contents," I went on. "Whatever they were, M. de Cocheforêt lost it and them at starting. A week ago he came back--unfortunately for himself--to seek them."

She was looking full in my face now. She seemed scarcely to breathe in the intensity of her surprise and expectation. "You had a search made, Mademoiselle," I continued quietly. "Your servants left no place unexplored. The paths, the roads, the very woods were ransacked. But in vain, because all the while the orange sachet lay whole and unopened in my pocket."

"No!" she cried impetuously. "You lie, Sir! The sachet was found, torn open, many leagues from this place!"

"Where I threw it, Mademoiselle," I replied, "that I might mislead your rascals and be free to return. Oh! believe me," I continued, letting something of myself, something of my triumph, appear at last in my voice. "You have made a mistake! You would have done better had you trusted me. I am no bundle of sawdust, Mademoiselle, but a man: a man with an arm to shield and a brain to serve, and--as I am going to teach you--a heart also!"

She shivered.

"In the orange-coloured sachet that you lost I believe there were eighteen stones of great value?"

She made no answer, but she looked at me as if I fascinated her. Her very breath seemed to pause and wait on my words. She was so little conscious of anything else, of anything outside ourselves, that a score of men might have come up behind her unseen and unnoticed.

A MASTER STROKE CONTINUE

I took from my breast a little packet wrapped in soft leather, and held it towards her. "Will you open this?" I said. "I believe it contains what you lost. That it contains all I will not answer, Mademoiselle, because I spilled the stones on the floor of my room, and I may have failed to find some. But the others can be recovered--I know where they are."

She took the packet slowly and began to unroll it, her fingers shaking. A few turns and the mild lustre of the stones made a kind of moonlight in her hands--such a shimmering glory of imprisoned light as has ruined many a woman and robbed many a man of his honour. Morbleu! as I looked at them--and as she stood looking at them in dull, entranced perplexity--I wondered how I had come to resist the temptation.

While I gazed her hands began to waver. "I cannot count," she muttered helplessly. "How many are there?"

"In all, eighteen.'

"They should be eighteen," she said.

She closed her hand on them with that, and opened it again, and did so twice, as if to reassure herself that the stones were real and that she was not dreaming. Then she turned to me with sudden fierceness, and I saw that her beautiful face, sharpened by the greed of possession, was grown as keen and vicious as before. "Well?" she muttered between her teeth. "Your price, man? Your price?"

"I am coming to it now, Mademoiselle," I said gravely. "It is a simple matter. You remember the afternoon when I followed you--clumsily and thoughtlessly perhaps--through the wood to restore these things? It seems about a month ago. I believe it happened the day before yesterday. You called me then some very harsh names, which I will not hurt you by repeating. The only price I ask for restoring your jewels is that you recall those names.

"How?" she muttered. "I do not understand."

I repeated my words very slowly. "The only price or reward I ask, Mademoiselle, is that you take back those names, and say that they were not deserved."

"And the jewels?" she exclaimed hoarsely.

"They are yours. They are nothing to me. Take them, and say that you do not think of me-- Nay, I cannot say the words, Mademoiselle."

"But there is something--else! What else?" she cried, her head thrown back, her eyes, bright as any wild animal's, searching mine. "Ha! my brother? What of him? What of him, Sir?"

"For him, Mademoiselle--I would prefer that you should tell me no more than I know already," I answered in a low voice. "I do not wish to be in that affair. But yes, there is one thing I have not mentioned. You are right."

She sighed so deeply that I caught the sound.

"It is," I continued slowly, "that you will permit me to remain at Cocheforêt for a few days, while the soldiers are here. I am told that there are twenty men and two officers quartered in your house. Your brother is away. I ask to be permitted, Mademoiselle, to take his place for the time, and to be privileged to protect your sister and yourself from insult. That is all."

She raised her hand to her head. After a long pause: "The frogs!" she muttered, "they croak! I cannot hear."

And then, to my surprise, she turned suddenly on her heel, and walked over the bridge, leaving me there. For a moment I stood aghast, peering after her shadowy figure, and wondering what had taken her. Then, in a minute or less, she came quickly back to me, and I understood. She was crying.

"M. de Barthe," she said, in a trembling voice, which told me that the victory was won. "Is there nothing else? Have you no other penance for me?"

"None, Mademoiselle."

She had drawn the shawl over her head, and I no longer saw her face. "That is all you ask?" she murmured.

"That is all I ask--now," I answered.

"It is granted," she said slowly and firmly. "Forgive me if I seem to speak lightly--if I seem to make little of your generosity or my shame; but I can say no more now. I am so deep in trouble and so gnawed by terror that--I cannot feel anything much to-night, either shame or gratitude. I am in a dream; God grant it may pass as a dream! We are sunk in trouble. But for you and what you have done, M. de Barthe--I--" she paused and I heard her fighting with the sobs which choked her--"forgive me.... I am overwrought. And my--my feet are cold," she added suddenly and irrelevantly. "Will you take me home?"

"Ah, Mademoiselle," I cried remorsefully, "I have been a beast! You are barefoot, and I have kept you here."

"It is nothing," she said in a voice which thrilled me. "My heart is warm, Monsieur--thanks to you. It is many hours since it has been as warm."

She stepped out of the shadow as she spoke--and there, the thing was done. As I had planned, so it had come about. Once more I was crossing the meadow in the dark to be received at Cocheforêt a welcome guest. The frogs croaked in the pool and a bat swooped round us in circles; and surely never--never, I thought, with a kind of exultation in my breast--had man been placed in a stranger position.

Somewhere in the black wood behind us--probably in the outskirts of the village--lurked M. de Cocheforêt. In the great house before us, outlined by a score of lighted windows, were the soldiers come from Auch to take him. Between the two, moving side by side in the darkness, in a silence which each found to be eloquent, were Mademoiselle and I: she who knew so much, I who knew all--all but one little thing!

We reached the house, and I suggested that she should steal in first by the way she had come out, and that I should wait a little and knock at the door when she had had time to explain matters to Clon.

"They do not let me see Clon," she answered slowly.

"Then your woman must tell him," I rejoined. "Or he may say something and betray me."

"They will not let our woman come to us."

"What?" I cried, astonished. "But this is infamous. You are not prisoners!"

Mademoiselle laughed harshly. "Are we not? Well, I suppose not; for if we wanted company, Captain Larolle said he would be delighted to see us-- in the parlour."

"He has taken your parlour?" I said.

"He and his lieutenant sit there. But I suppose we should be thankful," she added bitterly. "We have still our bed-rooms left to us."

"Very well," I said. "Then I must deal with Clon as I can. But I have still a favour to ask, Mademoiselle. It is only that you and your sister will descend to-morrow at your usual time. I shall be in the parlour."

"I would rather not," she said, pausing and speaking in a troubled voice.

"Are you afraid?"

"No, Monsieur; I am not afraid," she answered proudly. "But--"

"You will come?" I said.

She sighed before she spoke. At length, "Yes, I will come--if you wish it," she answered; and the next moment she was gone round the corner of the house, while I laughed to think of the excellent watch these gallant gentlemen were keeping. M. de Cocheforêt might have been with her in the garden, might have talked with her as I had talked, might have entered the house even, and passed under their noses scot-free. But that is the way of soldiers. They are always ready for the enemy, with drums beating and flags flying--at ten o'clock in the morning. But he does not always come at that hour.

I waited a little, and then I groped my way to the door, and knocked on it with the hilt of my sword. The dogs began to bark at the back, and the chorus of a drinking-song, which came fitfully from the east wing, ceased altogether. An inner door opened, and an angry voice, apparently an officer's, began to rate some one for not coming. Another moment, and a clamour of voices and footsteps seemed to pour into the hall, and fill it. I heard the bar jerked away, the door was flung open, and in a twinkling a lanthorn, behind which a dozen flushed visages were dimly seen, was thrust into my face.

"Why, who the fiend is this?" cried one, glaring at me in astonishment.

"Morbleu! It is the man!" another shrieked. "Seize him!"

In a moment half a dozen hands were laid on my shoulders, but I only bowed politely. "The officer, my friends," I said, "M. le Capitaine Larolle. Where is he?"

"Diable! but who are you, first?" the lanthorn-bearer retorted bluntly. He was a tall, lanky sergeant, with a sinister face.

"Well, I am not M. de Cocheforêt," I replied; "and that must satisfy you, my man. For the rest, if you do not fetch Captain Larolle at once and admit me, you will find the consequences inconvenient."

"Ho! ho!" he said, with a sneer. "You can crow, it seems. Well, come in."

They made way, and I walked into the hall, keeping my hat on. On the great hearth a fire had been kindled, but it had gone out. Three or four carbines stood against one wall, and beside them lay a heap of haversacks and some straw. A shattered stool, broken in a frolic, and half a dozen empty wine-skins strewed the floor, and helped to give the place an air of untidiness and disorder. I looked round with eyes of disgust, and my gorge rose. They had spilled oil, and the place reeked foully.

"Ventre bleu!" I said. "Is this conduct in a gentleman's house, you rascals? Ma vie! If I had you, I would send half of you to the wooden horse!"

They gazed at me open-mouthed. My arrogance startled them. The sergeant alone scowled. When he could find his voice for rage--

"This way!" he said. "We did not know a general officer was coming, or we would have been better prepared!" And muttering oaths under his breath, he led me down the well-known passage. At the door of the parlour he stopped. "Introduce yourself!" he said rudely. "And if you find the air warm, don't blame me!"

I raised the latch and went in. At a table in front of the hearth, half covered with glasses and bottles, sat two men playing hazard. The dice rang sharply as I entered, and he who had just thrown kept the box over them while he turned, scowling, to see who came in. He was a fair-haired, blonde man, large-framed and florid. He had put off his cuirass and boots, and his doublet showed frayed and stained where the armour had pressed on it. But otherwise he was in the extreme of last year's fashion. His deep cravat, folded over so that the laced ends drooped a little in front, was of the finest; his great sash of blue and silver was a foot wide. He had a little jewel in one ear, and his tiny beard was peaked à l'Espagnole. Probably when he turned he expected to see the sergeant, for at sight of me he rose slowly, leaving the dice still covered.

"What folly is this?" he cried wrathfully. "Here, Sergeant! Sergeant!-- without there! What the--! Who are you, Sir?"

"Captain Larolle," I said, uncovering politely, "I believe?"

"Yes, I am Captain Larolle," he retorted. "But who, in the fiend's name, are you? You are not the man we are after!"

"I am not M. Cocheforêt," I said coolly. "I am merely a guest in the house, M. le Capitaine. I have been enjoying Madame de Cocheforêt's hospitality for some time, but by an evil chance I was away when you arrived." And with that I walked to the hearth, and, gently pushing aside his great boots which stood there drying, kicked the logs into a blaze.

"Mille diables!" he whispered. And never did I see a man more confounded. But I affected to be taken up with his companion, a sturdy, white-mustachioed old veteran, who sat back in his chair, eyeing me, with swollen cheeks and eyes surcharged with surprise.

"Good evening, M. le Lieutenant," I said, bowing gravely. "It is a fine night."

Then the storm burst.

"Fine night!" the captain shrieked, finding his voice again. "Mille diables! Are you aware, Sir, that I am in possession of this house, and that no one harbours here without my permission? Guest! Hospitality! Lieutenant--call the guard! Call the guard!" he continued passionately. "Where is that ape of a sergeant?"

The lieutenant rose to obey, but I lifted my hand.

"Gently, gently, Captain," I said. "Not so fast! You seem surprised to see me here. Believe me, I am much more surprised to see you."

"Sacré!" he cried, recoiling at this fresh impertinence, while the lieutenant's eyes almost jumped out of his head.

But nothing moved me.

"Is the door closed?" I said sweetly. "Thank you; it is, I see. Then permit me to say again, gentlemen, that I am much more surprised to see you than you can be to see me. When Monseigneur the Cardinal honoured me by sending me from Paris to conduct this matter, he gave me the fullest--the fullest powers, M. le Capitaine--to see the affair to an end. I was not led to expect that my plans would be spoiled on the eve of success by the intrusion of half the garrison from Auch!"

"O ho!" the captain said softly--in a very different tone and with a very different face. "So you are the gentleman I heard of at Auch?"

"Very likely," I said drily. "But I am from Paris, not Auch."

"To be sure," he answered thoughtfully. "Eh, Lieutenant?"

"Yes, M. le Capitaine, no doubt," the inferior replied. And they both looked at one another, and then at me, in a way I did not understand.

"I think," said I, to clinch the matter, "that you have made a mistake, Captain; or the Commandant has. And it occurs to me that the Cardinal will not be best pleased."

"I hold the King's commission," he answered rather stiffly.

"To be sure," I replied. "But you see the Cardinal--"

"Ah, but the Cardinal--" he rejoined quickly; and then he stopped and shrugged his shoulders. And they both looked at me.

"Well?" I said.

"The King," he answered slowly.

"Tut-tut!" I exclaimed, spreading out my hands. "The Cardinal. Let us stick to him. You were saying?"

"Well, the Cardinal, you see--" And then again, after the same words, he stopped--stopped abruptly and shrugged his shoulders.

I began to suspect something. "If you have anything to say against Monseigneur," I answered, watching him narrowly, "say it. But take a word of advice. Don't let it go beyond the door of this room, my friend, and it will do you no harm."

"Neither here nor outside," he retorted, looking for a moment at his comrade. "Only I hold the King's commission. That is all. And I think enough. For the rest, will you throw a main? Good! Lieutenant, find a glass, and the gentleman a seat. And here, for my part, I will give you a toast. The Cardinal--whatever betide!"

I drank it, and sat down to play with him; I had not heard the music of the dice for a month, and the temptation was irresistible. But I was not satisfied. I called the mains and won his crowns,--he was a mere baby at the game,--but half my mind was elsewhere. There was something here I did not understand; some influence at work on which I had not counted; something moving under the surface as unintelligible to me as the soldiers' presence. Had the captain repudiated my commission altogether, and put me to the door or sent me to the guard-house, I could have followed that. But these dubious hints, this passive resistance, puzzled me. Had they news from Paris, I wondered. Was the King dead? or the Cardinal ill? I asked them. But they said no, no, no to all, and gave me guarded answers. And midnight found us still playing; and still fencing.

THE QUESTION

"Sweep the room, Monsieur? And remove this medley? But, M. le Capitaine--"

"The captain is at the village," I replied sternly. "And do you move! move, man, and the thing will be done while you are talking about it. Set the door into the garden open--so!"

"Certainly, it is a fine morning. And the tobacco of M. le Lieutenant-- But M. le Capitaine did not--"

"Give orders? Well, I give them!" I answered. "First of all, remove these beds. And bustle, man, bustle, or I will find something to quicken you."

In a moment-- "And M. le Capitaine's riding-boots?"

"Place them in the passage," I replied.

"Ohé! In the passage?" He paused, looking at them in doubt.

"Yes, booby; in the passage."

"And the cloaks, Monsieur?"

"There is a bush handy outside the window. Let them air."

"Ohé, the bush? Well, to be sure they are damp. But--yes, yes, Monsieur, it is done. And the holsters?"

"There also!" I said harshly. "Throw them out. Faugh! The place reeks of leather. Now, a clean hearth. And set the table before the open door, so that we may see the garden. So. And tell the cook that we shall dine at eleven, and that Madame and Mademoiselle will descend."

"Ohé! But M. le Capitaine ordered the dinner for half past eleven?"

"It must be advanced, then; and, mark you, my friend, if it is not ready when Madame comes down, you will suffer, and the cook too."

When he was gone on his errand, I looked round. What else was lacking? The sun shone cheerily on the polished floor; the air, freshened by the rain which had fallen in the night, entered freely through the open doorway. A few bees lingering with the summer hummed outside. The fire

77

crackled bravely; an old hound, blind and past work, lay warming its hide on the hearth. I could think of nothing more, and I stood and watched the man set out the table and spread the cloth. "For how many, Monsieur?" he asked, in a scared tone.

"For five," I answered; and I could not help smiling at myself. What would Zaton's say could it see Berault turned housewife? There was a white glazed cup--an old-fashioned piece of the second Henry's time--standing on a shelf. I took it down and put some late flowers in it, and set it in the middle of the table, and stood off myself to look at it. But a moment later, thinking I heard them coming, I hurried it away in a kind of panic, feeling on a sudden ashamed of the thing. The alarm proved to be false, however; and then again, taking another turn, I set the piece back. I had done nothing so foolish for--for more years than I liked to count.

But when Madame and Mademoiselle came, they had eyes neither for the flowers nor the room. They had heard that the captain was out beating the village and the woods for the fugitive, and where I had looked for a comedy I found a tragedy. Madame's face was so red with weeping that all her beauty was gone. She started and shook at the slightest sound, and, unable to find any words to answer my greeting, could only sink into a chair and sit crying silently.

Mademoiselle was in a mood scarcely more cheerful. She did not weep, but her manner was hard and fierce. She spoke absently and answered fretfully. Her eyes glittered, and she had the air of straining her ears continually to catch some dreaded sound. "There is no news, Monsieur?" she said, as she took her seat. And she shot a swift look at me.

"None, Mademoiselle."

"They are searching the village?"

"I believe so."

"Where is Clon?" This in a lower voice, and with a kind of shrinking in her face.

I shook my head. "I believe they have him confined somewhere. And Louis, too," I said, "But I have not seen either of them."

"And where are--? I thought these people would be here," she muttered. And she glanced askance at the two vacant places. The servant had brought in the meal.

"They will be here presently," I said coolly. "Let us make the most of the time. A little wine and food will do Madame good."

She smiled rather sadly. "I think we have changed places," she said; "and that you have turned host, and we guests."

"Let it be so," I said cheerfully. "I recommend some of this ragoût. Come, Mademoiselle; fasting can aid no one. A full meal has saved many a man's life."

It was clumsily said perhaps, for she shuddered and looked at me with a ghastly smile. But she persuaded her sister to taste something; and she took something on her own plate and raised her fork to her lips. But in a moment she laid it down again. "I cannot," she murmured. "I cannot swallow. Oh, my God, at this moment they may be taking him!"

I thought that she was about to burst into a passion of tears, and I repented that I had induced her to descend. But her self-control was not yet exhausted. By an effort painful to see, she recovered her composure. She took up her fork, and ate a few mouthfuls. Then she looked at me with a fierce under-look. "I want to see Clon," she whispered feverishly. The man who waited on us had left the room.

"He knows?" I said.

She nodded, her beautiful face strangely disfigured. Her closed teeth showed between her lips. Two red spots burned in her white cheeks, and she breathed quickly. I felt, as I looked at her, a sudden pain at my heart; and a shuddering fear, such as a man awaking to find himself falling over a precipice, might feel. How these women loved the man!

For a moment I could not speak. When I found my voice it sounded dry and husky. "He is a safe confidant," I muttered. "He can neither speak nor write, Mademoiselle."

"No, but--" and then her face became fixed. "They are coming," she whispered. "Hush!" She rose stiffly, and stood supporting herself by the table. "Have they--have they--found him?" she muttered. The woman by her side wept on, unconscious what was impending.

I heard the captain stumble far down the passage, and swear loudly; and I touched Mademoiselle's hand. "They have not!" I whispered. "All is well, Mademoiselle. Pray, pray calm yourself. Sit down, and meet them as if nothing were the matter. And your sister! Madame, Madame," I cried, almost harshly, "compose yourself. Remember that you have a part to play."

My appeal did something. Madame stifled her sobs. Mademoiselle drew a deep breath and sat down; and though she was still pale and still trembled, the worst was past.

And just in time. The door flew open with a crash. The captain stumbled into the room, swearing afresh. "Sacré nom du Diable!" he cried, his face crimson with rage. "What fool placed these things here? My boots? My--"

His jaw fell. He stopped on the word, stricken silent by the new aspect of the room, by the sight of the little party at the table, by all the changes I had worked. "Saint Siège!" I muttered. "What is this?" The lieutenant's grizzled face peering over his shoulder completed the picture.

"You are rather late, M. le Capitaine," I said cheerfully. "Madame's hour is eleven. But come, here are your seats waiting for you."

"Mille tonnerres!" he muttered, advancing into the room, and glaring at us.

"I am afraid the ragoût is cold," I continued, peering into the dish and affecting to see nothing. "The soup, however, has been kept hot by the fire. But I think you do not see Madame."

He opened his mouth to swear, but for the moment thought better of it. "Who--who put my boots in the passage?" he asked, his voice thick with rage. He did not bow to the ladies, or take any notice of their presence.

"One of the men, I suppose," I said indifferently. "Is anything missing?"

He glared at me. Then his cloak, spread outside, caught his eye. He strode through the door, saw his holsters lying on the grass, and other things strewn about. He came back. "Whose monkey game is this?" he snarled, and his face was very ugly. "Who is at the bottom of this? Speak, Sir, or I--"

"Tut-tut! the ladies!" I said. "You forget yourself, Monsieur."

"Forget myself?" he hissed, and this time he did not check his oath. "Don't talk to me of the ladies! Madame? Bah! Do you think, fool, that we are put into rebels' houses to bow and smile and take dancing lessons?"

"In this case a lesson in politeness were more to the point, Monsieur," I said sternly. And I rose.

"Was it by your orders that this was done?" he retorted, his brow black with passion. "Answer, will you?"

"It was!" I replied outright.

"Then take that!" he cried, dashing his hat violently in my face. "And come outside."

"With pleasure, Monsieur," I answered, bowing. "In one moment. Permit me to find my sword. I think it is in the passage."

I went thither to get it. When I returned I found that the two men were waiting for me in the garden, while the ladies had risen from the table and were standing near it with blanched faces. "You had better take your sister upstairs, Mademoiselle," I said gently, pausing a moment beside them. "Have no fear. All will be well."

"But what is it?" she answered, looking troubled. "It was so sudden. I am--I did not understand. You quarrelled so quickly."

"It is very simple," I answered, smiling. "M. le Capitaine insulted you yesterday; he will pay for it to-day. That is all. Or, not quite all," I continued, dropping my voice and speaking in a different tone. "His removal may help you, Mademoiselle. Do you understand? I think that there will be no more searching to-day."

She uttered an exclamation, grasping my arm and peering into my face. "You will kill him?" she muttered.

I nodded. "Why not?" I said.

She caught her breath and stood with one hand clasped to her bosom, gazing at me with parted lips, the blood mounting to her cheeks. Gradually the flush melted into a fierce smile. "Yes, yes, why not?" she repeated, between her teeth. "Why not?" She had her hand on my arm, and I felt her fingers tighten until I could have winced. "Why not? So you planned this--for us, Monsieur?"

I nodded.

"But can you?"

"Safely," I said; then, muttering to her to take her sister upstairs, I turned towards the garden. My foot was already on the threshold, and I was composing my face to meet the enemy, when I heard a movement behind me. The next moment her hand was on my arm. "Wait! Wait a moment! Come back!" she panted. I turned. The smile and flush had vanished; her face was pale. "No!" she said abruptly. "I was wrong! I will not have it. I will have no part in it! You planned it last night, M. de Barthe. It is murder."

"Mademoiselle!" I exclaimed, wondering. "Murder? Why? It is a duel."

"It is murder," she answered persistently. "You planned it last night. You said so."

"But I risk my own life," I replied sharply.

"Nevertheless--I will have no part in it," she answered more faintly. "It will bring no good." She was trembling with agitation. Her eyes avoided mine.

"On my shoulders be it then!" I replied stoutly. "It is too late, Mademoiselle, to go back. They are waiting for me. Only, before I go, let me beg of you to retire."

And I turned from her, and went out, wondering and thinking. First, that women were strange things. Secondly--murder? Merely because I had planned the duel and provoked the quarrel! Never had I heard anything so preposterous. Grant it, and dub every man who kept his honour with his hands a Cain--and a good many branded faces would be seen in some streets. I laughed at the fancy, as I strode down the garden walk.

And yet, perhaps, I was going to do a foolish thing. The lieutenant would still be here: a hard, bitter man, of stiffer stuff than his captain. And the troopers. What if, when I had killed their leader, they made the place too hot for me, Monseigneur's commission notwithstanding? I should look silly, indeed, if on the eve of success I were driven from the place by a parcel of jack-boots.

I liked the thought so little that I hesitated Yet it seemed too late to retreat. The captain and the lieutenant were waiting in a little open space fifty yards from the house, where a narrower path crossed the broad walk, down which I had first seen Mademoiselle and her sister pacing. The captain had removed his doublet, and stood in his shirt leaning against the sundial, his head bare and his sinewy throat uncovered. He had drawn his rapier and stood pricking the ground impatiently. I marked his strong and nervous frame and his sanguine air: and twenty years earlier the sight might have damped me. But no thought of the kind entered my head now, and though I felt with each moment greater reluctance to engage, doubt of the issue had no place in my calculations.

I made ready slowly, and would gladly, to gain time, have found some fault with the place. But the sun was sufficiently high to give no advantage to either. The ground was good, the spot well chosen. I could find no excuse to put off the man, and I was about to salute him and fall to work, when a thought crossed my mind.

"One moment!" I said. "Supposing I kill you, M. le Capitaine, what becomes of your errand here?"

"Don't trouble yourself," he answered, with a sneer--he had misread my slowness and hesitation. "It will not happen, Monsieur. And in any case the thought need not harass you. I have a lieutenant."

"Yes, but what of my mission?" I replied bluntly. "I have no lieutenant."

"You should have thought of that before you interfered with my boots," he retorted, with contempt.

"True," I said, overlooking his manner. "But better late than never. I am not sure, now I think of it, that my duty to Monseigneur will let me fight."

"You will swallow the blow?" he cried, spitting on the ground offensively. "Diable!" And the lieutenant, standing on one side with his hands behind him and his shoulders squared, laughed grimly.

"I have not made up my mind," I answered irresolutely.

"Well, nom de Dieu! make it up," the captain replied, with an ugly sneer. He took a swaggering step this way and that, playing his weapon. "I am afraid, Lieutenant, there will be no sport to-day," he continued, in a loud aside. "Our cock has but a chicken heart."

"Well!" I said coolly, "I do not know what to do. Certainly it is a fine day, and a fair piece of ground. And the sun stands well. But I have not much to gain by killing you, M. le Capitaine, and it might get me into an awkward fix. On the other hand, it would not hurt me to let you go."

"Indeed?" he said contemptuously, looking at me as I should look at a lacquey.

"No!" I replied. "For if you were to say that you had struck Gil de Berault, and left the ground with a whole skin, no one would believe you."

"Gil de Berault!" he exclaimed, frowning.

"Yes, Monsieur," I replied suavely. "At your service. You did not know my name?"

"I thought your name was De Barthe," he said. His voice sounded queerly; and he waited for the answer with parted lips, and a shadow in his eyes which I had seen in men's eyes before.

"No," I said. "That was my mother's name, I took it for this occasion only."

His florid cheek lost a shade of its colour, and he bit his lips as he glanced at the lieutenant, trouble in his eyes. I had seen these signs before, and knew them, and I might have cried "Chicken-heart!" in my turn; but I had not made a way of escape for him--before I declared myself--for nothing, and I held to my purpose. "I think you will allow now," I said grimly, "that it will not harm me even if I put up with a blow!"

"M. de Berault's courage is known," he muttered.

"And with reason," I said. "That being so, suppose we say this day three months, M. le Capitaine? The postponement to be for my convenience."

He caught the lieutenant's eye, and looked down sullenly, the conflict in his mind as plain as daylight. He had only to insist, and I must fight; and if by luck or skill he could master me, his fame as a duellist would run, like a ripple over water, through every garrison town in France and make him a name even in Paris. On the other side were the imminent peril of death, the gleam of cold steel already in fancy at his breast, the loss of life and sunshine, and the possibility of a retreat with honour, if without glory. I read his face, and knew before he spoke what he would do.

"It appears to me that the burden is with you," he said huskily; "but for my part, I am satisfied."

"Very well," I said, "I take the burden. Permit me to apologize for having caused you to strip unnecessarily. Fortunately the sun is shining."

"Yes," he said gloomily. And he took his clothes from the sundial, and began to put them on. He had expressed himself satisfied; but I knew that he was feeling very ill-satisfied with himself, and I was not surprised when he presently said abruptly and almost rudely, "There is one thing I think we must settle here."

"What is that?" I asked.

"Our positions," he blurted out. "Or we shall cross one another again within the hour."

"Umph! I am not quite sure that I understand," I said.

"That is precisely what I don't do--understand!" he retorted, in a tone of surly triumph. "Before I came on this duty, I was told that there was a gentleman here, bearing sealed orders from the Cardinal to arrest M. de Cocheforêt; and I was instructed to avoid collision with him so far as might be possible. At first I took you for the gentleman. But the plague take me if I understand the matter now."

"Why not?" I said coldly.

"Because--well, the matter is in a nutshell!" he answered impetuously. "Are you here on behalf of Madame de Cocheforêt to shield her husband? Or are you here to arrest him? That is what I don't understand, M. de Berault."

"If you mean, am I the Cardinal's agent--I am!" I answered sternly.

"To arrest M. de Cocheforêt?"

"To arrest M. de Cocheforêt."

"Well--you surprise me," he said.

Only that; but he spoke so drily that I felt the blood rush to my face. "Take care, Monsieur," I said severely. "Do not presume too far on the inconvenience to which your death might put me."

He shrugged his shoulders. "No offence!" he said. "But you do not seem, M. de Berault, to comprehend the difficulty. If we do not settle things now, we shall be bickering twenty times a day!"

"Well, what do you want?" I asked impatiently.

"Simply to know how you are going to proceed. So that our plans may not clash."

"But surely, M. le Capitaine, that is my affair!" I replied.

"The clashing?" he answered bitterly. Then he waved aside my wrath. "Pardon," he said, "the point is simply this: How do you propose to find him if he is here?"

"That again is my affair," I answered.

He threw up his hands in despair; but in a moment his place was taken by an unexpected disputant. The lieutenant, who had stood by all the time, listening and tugging at his grey moustache, suddenly spoke. "Look here, M. de Berault," he said, confronting me roughly, "I do not fight duels. I am from the ranks. I proved my courage at Montauban in '21, and my honour is good enough to take care of itself. So I say what I like, and I ask you plainly what M. le Capitaine doubtless has in his mind but does not ask: Are you running with the hare and hunting with the hounds in this matter? In other words, have you thrown up Monseigneur's commission in all but name and become Madame's ally; or--it is the only other alternative--are you getting at the man through the women?"

"You villain!" I cried, glaring at him in such a rage and fury I could scarcely get the words out. This was plain speaking with a vengeance! "How dare you! How dare you say that I am false to the hand that pays me?"

I thought he would blench, but he did not. He stood up stiff as a poker. "I do not say; I ask!" he replied, facing me squarely, and slapping his fist into his open hand to drive home his words the better. "I ask you whether you are playing the traitor to the Cardinal? Or to these two women? It is a simple question."

I fairly choked. "You impudent scoundrel," I said.

"Steady, steady!" he replied. "Pitch sticks where it belongs. But that is enough. I see which it is, M. le Capitaine; this way a moment, by your leave."

And in a very cavalier way he took his officer by the arm, and drew him into a side-walk, leaving me to stand in the sun, bursting with anger and spleen. The gutter-bred rascal! That such a man should insult me, and with impunity! In Paris I might have made him fight, but here it was impossible. I was still foaming with rage when they returned.

"We have come to a determination," the lieutenant said, tugging his grey mustachios and standing like a ramrod. "We shall leave you the house and Madame, and you can take your line to find the man. For ourselves, we shall draw off our men to the village, and we shall take our line. That is all, M. le Capitaine, is it not?"

"I think so," the captain muttered, looking anywhere but at me.

"Then we bid you good-day, Monsieur," the lieutenant added. And in a moment he turned his companion round, and the two retired up the walk to the house, leaving me to look after them in a black fit of rage and incredulity. At the first flush there was something so offensive in the manner of their going that anger had the upper hand. I thought of the lieutenant's words, and I cursed him to hell with a sickening consciousness that I should not forget them in a hurry: "Was I playing the traitor to the Cardinal or to these women--which?" Mon Dieu! if ever question--but there! some day I would punish him. And the captain? I could put an end to his amusement, at any rate; and I would. Doubtless among the country bucks of Auch he lorded it as a chief provincial bully, but I would cut his comb for him some fine morning behind the barracks.

And then, as I grew cooler I began to wonder why they were going, and what they were going to do. They might be already on the track, or have the information they required under hand; in that case I could understand the movement. But if they were still searching vaguely, uncertain whether their quarry were in the neighbourhood or not, and uncertain how long they might have to stay, it seemed incredible that soldiers should move from good quarters to bad without motive.

I wandered down the garden thinking sullenly of this, and pettishly cutting off the heads of the flowers with my sheathed sword. After all, if they found and arrested the man, what then? I should have to make my peace with the Cardinal as I best might. He would have gained his point, but not through me, and I should have to look to myself. On the other hand, if I anticipated them--and, as a fact, I felt that I could lay my hand on the fugitive within a few hours--there would come a time when I must face Mademoiselle.

A little while back that had not seemed so difficult a thing. From the day of our first meeting--and in a higher degree since that afternoon when she had lashed me with her scorn--my views of her, and my feelings towards her, had been strangely made up of antagonism and sympathy; of repulsion, because in her past and present she was so different from me; of yearning, because she was a woman and friendless. Then I had duped her and bought her confidence by returning the jewels, and in a measure I had sated my vengeance; and then, as a consequence, sympathy had again begun to get the better, until now I hardly knew my own mind or what I intended. I did not know, in fact, what I intended. I stood there in the garden with that conviction suddenly new-born in my mind; and then, in a moment, I heard her step and turned to find her behind me.

Her face was like April, smiles breaking through her tears. As she stood with a tall hedge of sunflowers behind her, I started to see how beautiful she was. "I am here in search of you, M. de Barthe," she said, colouring slightly, perhaps because my eyes betrayed my thought, "to thank you. You have not fought, and yet you have conquered. My woman has just been with me, and she tells me that they are going!"

"Going?" I said. "Yes, Mademoiselle, they are leaving the house."

She did not understand my reservation. "What magic have you used?" she said, almost gaily--it was wonderful how hope had changed her. "Moreover, I am curious to learn how you managed to avoid fighting."

"After taking a blow?" I said bitterly.

"Monsieur, I did not mean that," she said reproachfully. But her face clouded. I saw that, viewed in this light--in which I suppose she had not seen it--the matter perplexed her still more.

I took a sudden resolution. "Have you ever heard, Mademoiselle," I said gravely, plucking off while I spoke the dead leaves from a plant beside me, "of a gentleman by name De Berault? Known in Paris, so I have heard, by the sobriquet of the Black Death?"

"The duellist?" she answered, in wonder. "Yes, I have heard of him. He killed a young gentleman of this province at Nancy two years back. It was a sad story," she continued, shuddering, "of a dreadful man. God keep our friends from such!"

"Amen!" I said quietly. But, in spite of myself, I could not meet her eyes.

"Why?" she answered, quickly taking alarm at my silence. "What of him, M. de Barthe? Why have you mentioned him?"

"Because he is here, Mademoiselle."

"Here?" she exclaimed.

"Yes, Mademoiselle," I answered soberly. "I am he."

CLON

"You!" she cried, in a voice which pierced me, "You--M. de Berault? Impossible!" But, glancing askance at her.--I could not face her,--I saw that the blood had left her cheeks.

"Yes, Mademoiselle," I answered, in a low voice. "De Barthe was my mother's name. When I came here, a stranger, I took it that I might not be known; that I might again speak to a good woman and not see her shrink. That--but why trouble you with all this?" I continued proudly, rebelling against her silence, her turned shoulder, her averted face. "You asked me, Mademoiselle, how I could take a blow and let the striker go. I have answered. It is the one privilege M. de Berault possesses."

"Then," she replied quickly, but almost in a whisper, "if I were M. de Berault, I would use it, and never fight again."

"In that event, Mademoiselle," I answered cynically, "I should lose my men friends as well as my women friends. Like Monseigneur, the Cardinal, I rule by fear."

She shuddered, either at the name or at the idea my words called up, and, for a moment, we stood awkwardly silent. The shadow of the sundial fell between us; the garden was still; here and there a leaf fluttered slowly down, or a seed fell. With each instant of silence I felt the gulf between us growing wider, I felt myself growing harder; I mocked at her past, which was so unlike mine; I mocked at mine, and called it fate. I was on the point of turning from her with a bow--and a furnace in my breast--when she spoke.

"There is a late rose lingering there," she said, a slight tremor in her voice. "I cannot reach it. Will you pluck it for me, M. de Berault?"

I obeyed her, my hand trembling, my face on fire. She took the rose from me, and placed it in the bosom of her dress. And I saw that her hand trembled too, and that her cheek was dark with blushes.

She turned at once, and began to walk towards the house. Presently she spoke. "Heaven forbid that I should misjudge you a second time!" she said, in a low voice. "And, after all, who am I that I should judge you at all? An hour ago, I would have killed that man had I possessed the power."

"You repented, Mademoiselle," I said huskily. I could scarcely speak.

"Do you never repent?"

"Yes. But too late, Mademoiselle."

"Perhaps it is never too late," she answered softly.

"Alas, when a man is dead--"

"You may rob a man of more than life!" she replied with energy, stopping me by a gesture. "If you have never robbed a man--or a woman-- of honour! If you have never ruined boy or girl, M. de Berault! If you have never pushed another into the pit and gone by it yourself! If--but for murder? Listen. You may be a Romanist, but I am a Huguenot, and have read. 'Thou shalt not kill!' it is written; and the penalty, 'By man shall thy blood be shed!' But, 'If you cause one of these little ones to offend, it were better for you that a mill-stone were hanged about your neck, and that you were cast into the depths of the sea."

"Mademoiselle, you are too merciful," I muttered.

"I need mercy myself," she answered, sighing. "And I have had few temptations. How do I know what you have suffered?"

"Or done!" I said, almost rudely.

"Where a man has not lied, nor betrayed, nor sold himself or others," she answered firmly, but in a low tone, "I think I can forgive all else. I can better put up with force," she added, smiling sadly, "than with fraud."

Ah, Dieu! I turned away my face that she might not see how it paled, how I winced; that she might not guess how her words, meant in mercy, stabbed me to the heart. And yet, then, for the first time, while viewing in all its depth and width the gulf which separated us, I was not hardened; I was not cast back on myself. Her gentleness, her pity, her humility, softened me, while they convicted me. My God! How could I do that which I had come to do? How could I stab her in the tenderest part, how could I inflict on her that rending pang, how could I meet her eyes, and stand before her, a Caliban, a Judas, the vilest, lowest, basest thing she could conceive?

I stood, a moment, speechless and disordered; stunned by her words, by my thoughts--as I have seen a man stand when he has lost his all, his last, at the tables. Then I turned to her; and for an instant I thought that my tale was told already. I thought that she had pierced my disguise, for her face was aghast, stricken with sudden fear. Then I saw that she was not looking at me, but beyond me, and I turned quickly and saw a servant hurrying from the house to us. It was Louis. His face, it was, had frightened her. His eyes were staring, his hair waved, his cheeks were flabby with dismay. He breathed as if he had been running.

"What is it?" Mademoiselle cried, while he was still some way off. "Speak, man. My sister? Is she--"

"Clon," he gasped.

The name changed her to stone. "Clon?" she muttered. "What of him?"

"In the village!" Louis panted, his tongue stuttering with terror. "They are flogging him! They are killing him, Mademoiselle! To make him tell!"

Mademoiselle grasped the sundial and leant against it, her face colourless, and, for an instant, I thought that she was fainting. "Tell?" I said mechanically. "But he cannot tell. He is dumb, man."

"They will make him guide them," Louis groaned, covering his ears with his shaking hands, his face like paper. "And his cries! Oh, Monsieur, go!" he continued, suddenly appealing to me, in a thrilling tone. "Save him. All through the wood I heard them. It was horrible! horrible!"

Mademoiselle uttered a low moan, and I turned to support her, thinking each second to see her fall. But with a sudden movement she straightened herself, and, slipping by me, with eyes which seemed to see nothing, she started swiftly down the walk towards the meadow gate.

I ran after her, but, taken by surprise as I was, it was only by a great effort I reached the gate before her, and, thrusting myself in the road, barred the way. "Let me pass!" she panted fiercely, striving to thrust me on one side. "Out of my way, Sir! I am going to the village."

"You are not going to the village," I said sternly. "Go back to the house, Mademoiselle, and at once."

"My servant!" she wailed. "Let me go! Oh, let me go! Do you think I can rest here while they torture him? He cannot speak, and they--they--"

"Go back, Mademoiselle," I said, cutting her short, with decision. "You would only make matters worse! I will go myself, and what one man can do against many, I will! Louis, give your mistress your arm and take her to the house. Take her to Madame."

"But you will go?" she cried. Before I could stay her--I swear I would have done so if I could--she raised my hand and carried it to her trembling lips. "You will go! Go and stop them! Stop them," she continued, in a tone which stirred my heart, "and Heaven reward you, Monsieur!"

I did not answer; nor did I once look back, as I crossed the meadow; but I did not look forward either. Doubtless it was grass I trod; doubtless the wood was before me with the sun shining aslant on it, and behind me the house with a flame here and there on the windows. But I went in a dream, among shadows; with a racing pulse, in a glow from head to heel; conscious of nothing but the touch of Mademoiselle's warm lips, seeing neither meadows nor house, nor even the dark fringe of wood before me, but only Mademoiselle's passionate face. For the moment I was drunk: drunk with that to which I had been so long a stranger, with that which a man may scorn for years, to find it at last beyond his reach--drunk with the touch of a good woman's lips.

I passed the bridge in this state; and my feet were among the brushwood before the heat and fervour in which I moved found on a sudden their direction. Something began to penetrate to my veiled senses--a hoarse inarticulate cry, now deep, now shrilling horribly, which seemed to fill the wood. It came at intervals of half a minute or so, and made the flesh creep, it was so full of dumb pain, of impotent wrestling, of unspeakable agony. I am a man and have seen things. I saw the Concini beheaded, and Chalais ten years later--they gave him thirty-four blows; and when I was a boy I escaped from the college and viewed from a great distance Ravaillac torn by horses--that was in the year ten. But the horrible cries I now heard filled me, perhaps because I was alone and fresh from the sight of Mademoiselle, with loathing that was intense. The very wood, though the sun wanted an hour of setting, seemed to grow dark. I ran on through it, cursing, until the hovels of the village at length came in sight. Again the shriek rose, a pulsing horror, and this time I could hear the lash fall on the sodden flesh, I could see in fancy the strong man, trembling, quivering, straining against his bonds. And then, in a moment, I was in the street, and, as the scream once more tore the air, I dashed round the corner by the inn, and came upon them.

I did not look at him. I saw Captain Larolle and the lieutenant, and a ring of troopers, and one man, bare-armed, teasing out with his fingers the thongs of a whip. The thongs dripped blood, and the sight fired the mine. The rage I had suppressed when the lieutenant bearded me earlier in the afternoon, the passion with which Mademoiselle's distress had filled my breast, at last found vent. I sprang through the line of soldiers, and striking the man with the whip a buffet between the shoulders, which hurled him breathless to the ground, I turned on the leaders. "You devils!" I cried. "Shame on you! The man is dumb! I tell you, if I had ten men with me, I would sweep you and your scum out of the village with broomsticks. Lay on another lash," I continued recklessly, "and I will see if you or the Cardinal be the stronger."

The lieutenant glared at me, his grey moustache bristling, his eyes almost starting from his head. Some of the troopers laid their hands on their swords, but no one moved, and only the captain spoke. "Mille diables!" he swore. "What is all this about? Are you mad, Sir?"

"Mad or sane!" I cried, still in a fury. "Lay on another lash, and you shall repent it."

"I?"

"Yes, you!"

For an instant there was a pause of astonishment. Then to my surprise the captain laughed--laughed loudly. "Very heroic!" he said. "Quite magnificent, M. le Chevalier-errant. But you see, unfortunately, you come too late!"

"Too late!" I said incredulously.

"Yes, too late," he replied, with a mocking smile. And the lieutenant grinned too. "You see the man has just confessed. We have only been giving him an extra touch or two, to impress his memory, and save us the trouble of tying him up again."

"I don't believe it," I said bluntly--but I felt the check, and fell to earth. "The man cannot speak."

"No, but he has managed to tell us that he will guide us to the place we want," the captain answered drily. "The whip, if it cannot find a man a tongue, can find him wits. What is more, I think, he will keep his word," he continued, with a hideous smile. "For I warn him that if he does not, all your heroics shall not save him! He is a rebel dog, and known to us of old, and I will flay his back to the bones--ay, until we can see his heart beating through his ribs--but I will have what I want--in your teeth, too, you d--d meddler."

"Steady, steady!" I said, somewhat sobered. I saw that he was telling me the truth. "He is going to take you to M. de Cocheforêt's hiding-place, is he?"

"Yes, he is!" the captain retorted offensively. "Have you any objection to make to that, Master Spy?"

"None," I replied. "But I shall go with you. And if you live three months, I shall kill you for that name--behind the barracks at Auch, M. le Capitaine."

He changed colour, but he answered me boldly enough. "I don't know that you will go with us. That is as we please," he continued, with a snarl.

"I have the Cardinal's orders," I said sternly.

"The Cardinal?" he exclaimed, stung to fury by this repetition of the name. "The Cardinal be--"

But the lieutenant laid his hands on his lips, and stopped him. "Hush!" he said. Then more quietly, "Your pardon, M. le Capitaine. Shall I give orders to the men to fall in?"

The captain nodded sullenly.

"Take him down!" the lieutenant ordered, in his harsh, monotonous voice. "Throw his blouse over him, and tie his hands. And do you two, Paul and Lebrun, guard him. Michel, bring the whip, or he may forget how it tastes. Sergeant, choose four good men and dismiss the rest to their quarters."

"Shall we need the horses?" the sergeant asked.

"I don't know," the captain answered peevishly. "What does the rogue say?"

The lieutenant stepped up to him. "Listen!" he said grimly. "Nod if you mean yes, and shake your head if you mean no. And have a care you answer truly. Is it more than a mile to this place? The place you know of?"

They had loosened the poor wretch's fastenings, and covered his back. He stood leaning against the wall, his mouth still panting, the sweat running down his hollow cheeks; his sunken eyes were closed; a quiver now and again ran through his frame. The lieutenant repeated his question, and, getting no answer, looked round for orders. The captain met the look, and crying savagely, "Answer, will you, you mute!" struck the half-swooning miserable across the back with his switch. The effect was magical. Covered, as his shoulders were, the man sprang erect with a shriek of pain, raising his chin, and hollowing his back; and in that attitude stood an instant with starting eyes, gasping for breath. Then he sank back against the wall, moving his mouth spasmodically. His face was the colour of lead.

"Diable! I think we have gone too far with him!" the captain muttered.

"Bring some wine!" the lieutenant replied. "Quick with it!"

I looked on, burning with indignation, and wondering besides what would come of this. If the man took them to the place, and they succeeded in seizing, Cocheforêt, there was an end of the matter as far as I was concerned. It was off my shoulders, and I might leave the village when I pleased; nor was it likely--since he would have his man, though not through me--that the Cardinal would refuse me an amnesty. On the whole, I thought that I would prefer that things should take that course; and assuming the issue, I began to wonder whether in that event it would be necessary that Madame should know the truth. I had a kind of a vision of a reformed Berault, dead to play and purging himself at a distance from Zaton's, winning, perhaps, a name In the Italian war, and finally--but, pshaw! I was a fool.

However, be that as it might, it was essential that I should see the arrest made; and I waited patiently while they revived the tortured man, and made their dispositions. These took some time; so that the sun was down, and it was growing dusk, when we marched out, Clon going first, supported by his two guards, the captain and I following,--abreast, and eyeing one another suspiciously,--the lieutenant, with the sergeant and five troopers, bringing up the rear. Clon moved slowly, moaning from time to time, and but for the aid given him by the two men with him, must have sunk down again and again.

He went out between two houses close to the inn, and struck a narrow track, scarcely discernible, which ran behind other houses, and then plunged into the thickest part of the wood. A single person, traversing the covert, might have made such a track; or pigs, or children. But it was the first idea that occurred to us, and it put us all on the alert. The captain carried a cocked pistol, I held my sword drawn, and kept a watchful eye on him; and the deeper the dusk fell in the wood, the more cautiously we went, until at last we came out with a sort of jump into a wider and lighter path.

I looked up and down it, and saw before me a wooden bridge, and an open meadow, lying cold and grey in the twilight; and I stood in astonishment. It was the old path to the Château! I shivered at the thought that he was going to take us there, to the house--to Mademoiselle!

The captain also recognised the place, and swore aloud. But the dumb man went on unheeding, until he reached the wooden bridge. There he paused as if in doubt, and looked towards the dark outline of the building, which was just visible, one faint light twinkling sadly in the west wing. As the captain and I pressed up behind him, he raised his hands and seemed to wring them towards the house.

"Have a care!" the captain growled. "Play me no tricks, or--" But he did not finish the sentence; for Clon turned back from the bridge, and, entering the wood on the left hand, began to ascend the bank of the stream. We had not gone a hundred yards before the ground grew rough, and the undergrowth thick; and yet through all ran a kind of path which enabled us to advance, dark as it was growing. Very soon the bank on which we moved began to rise above the water, and grew steep and rugged. We turned a shoulder, where the stream swept round a curve, and saw we were in the mouth of a small ravine, dark and steep-walled. The water brawled along the bottom, over boulders and through chasms. In front, the slope on which we stood shaped itself into a low cliff; but half-way between its summit and the water, a ledge, or narrow terrace, running along the face, was dimly visible.

"Ten to one, a cave!" the captain muttered. "It is a likely place."

"And an ugly one!" I sneered. "Which one to ten might safely hold for hours!"

"If the ten had no pistols--yes!" he answered viciously. "But you see we have. Is he going that way?"

He was. "Lieutenant," Larolle said, turning and speaking in a low voice, though the chafing of the stream below us covered ordinary sounds, "shall we light the lanthorns, or press on while there is still a glimmering of day?"

"On, I should say, M. le Capitaine," the lieutenant answered. "Prick him in the back if he falters. I will warrant he has a tender place or two!" the brute added, with a chuckle.

The captain gave the word, and we moved forward; it being very evident now that the cliff-path was our destination. It was possible for the eye to follow the track all the way to it through rough stones and brushwood; and though Clon climbed feebly and with many groans, two minutes saw us step on to it. It did not turn out to be the perilous place it looked at a distance. The ledge, grassy and terrace-like, sloped slightly downwards and outwards, and in parts was slippery; but it was as wide as a highway, and the fall to the water did not exceed thirty feet. Even in such a dim light as now displayed it to us, and by increasing the depth and unseen dangers of the gorge, gave a kind of impressiveness to our movements, a nervous woman need not have feared to breast it. I wondered how often Mademoiselle had passed along it with her milk-pitcher.

"I think we have him now!" Captain Larolle muttered, twisting his mustachios, and looking round to make his last dispositions. "Paul and Lebrun, see that your man makes no noise. Sergeant, come forward with your carbine, but do not fire without orders. Now, silence, all, and close up, Lieutenant. Forward!"

We advanced about a hundred paces, keeping the cliff on our left, then turned a shoulder, and saw, a few paces in front of us, a black blotch standing out from the grey duskiness of the cliff-side. The prisoner stopped, and raising his bound hands pointed to it.

"There?" the captain whispered, pressing forward. "Is that the place?"

Clon nodded. The captain's voice shook with excitement. "You two remain here with him!" he muttered, in a low tone. "Sergeant, come forward with me. Now, are you ready? Forward!"

He and the sergeant passed quickly, one on either side of Clon and his guards. The path was narrow here, and the captain passed outside. The eyes of all but one were on the black blotch, the hollow in the cliff-side, and no one saw exactly what happened. But somehow, as the captain passed abreast of him, the prisoner thrust back his guards, and springing sideways, flung his unbound arms round Larolle's body, and in an instant swept him, shouting, to the verge of the precipice.

It was done in a moment. By the time the lieutenant's startled wits and eyes were back, the two were already tottering on the edge, looking in the gloom like one dark form. The sergeant, who was the first to find his head, levelled his carbine; but as the wrestlers twirled and twisted, the captain shrieking out oaths and threats, the mute silent as death, it was impossible to see which was which; and the sergeant lowered his gun again, while the men held back nervously. The ledge sloped steeply there; the edge was vague; already the two seemed to be wrestling in mid-air,--and the mute was a man beyond hope or fear.

That moment of hesitation was fatal. Clon's long arms were round the other's arms, crushing them into his ribs; Clon's skull-like face grinned hate into the other's eyes; his long limbs curled round him like the folds of a snake. Suddenly Larolle's strength gave way. "Damn you all! Why don't you--Mercy! mercy!" came in a last scream from his lips; and then, as the lieutenant, taken aback before, sprang forward to his aid, the two toppled over the edge, and in a second hurtled out of sight.

"Mon Dieu!" the lieutenant cried, in horror. The answer was a dull splash in the depths below.

He flung up his arms. "Water!" he said. "Quick, men, get down! We may save him yet! They have fallen into water!"

But there was no path, and night was come, and the men's nerves were shaken. The lanthorns had to be lit, and the way to be retraced; and by the time we reached the dark pool which lay below, the last bubbles were gone from the surface, the last ripples had beaten themselves out against the banks. True, the pool still rocked sullenly, and the yellow light showed a man's hat floating, and near it a glove three parts submerged. But that was all. The mute's dying grip had known no loosening, nor his hate any fear. Later, I heard that when they dragged the two out next day, his fingers were in the other's eye-sockets, his teeth in his throat. If ever man found death sweet, it was he.

As we turned slowly from the black water, some shuddering, some crossing themselves, the lieutenant looked vengefully at me. "Curse you!" he said, in sudden fury. "I believe you are glad!"

"He deserved his fate," I answered coldly. "Why should I pretend to be sorry? It was now or in three months. And for the other poor devil's sake I am glad."

He glared at me a moment, in speechless anger. At last, "I should like to have you tied up!" he said, between his teeth.

"I should have thought that you had had enough of tying up for one day!" I retorted. "But there; it comes of making officers out of the canaille. Dogs love blood. The teamster must still lash something, if he can no longer lash his horses."

We were back, a sombre little procession, at the wooden bridge, when I said this. He stopped suddenly. "Very well," he replied, nodding viciously, "That decides me. Sergeant, light me this way with a lanthorn. The rest of you to the village. Now, Master Spy," he continued, glancing at me with gloomy spite, "your road is my road. I think I know how to cook your goose."

I shrugged my shoulders in disdain, and together, the sergeant leading the way with the light, we crossed the meadow, and passed through the gate where Mademoiselle had kissed my hand, and up the ghostly walk between the rosebushes. I wondered uneasily what the lieutenant would be at, and what he intended; but the lanthorn light which now fell on the ground at our feet, and now showed one of us to the other, high-lit in a frame of blackness, discovered nothing in his grizzled face but settled hostility. He wheeled at the end of the walk to go to the main door; but as he did so, I saw the flutter of a white skirt by the stone seat against the house, and I stepped that way. "Mademoiselle," I said softly, "is it you?"

"Clon?" she muttered, her voice quivering. "What of him?"

"He is past pain," I answered gently. "He is dead, but in his own way. Take comfort, Mademoiselle." And then before I could say more, the lieutenant with his sergeant and light were at my elbow. He saluted Mademoiselle roughly. She looked at him with shuddering abhorrence.

"Are you come to flog me, Sir?" she said icily. "Is it not enough that you have murdered my servant?"

"On the contrary, it was he killed my captain," the lieutenant answered, in another tone than I had expected. "If your servant is dead, so is my comrade."

She looked with startled eyes, not at him, but at me. "What! Captain Larolle?" she muttered.

I nodded.

"How?" she asked.

"Clon flung the captain and himself into the river-pool," I explained, in a low voice. "The pool above the bridge."

She uttered an exclamation of awe, and stood silent. But her lips moved; I think she was praying for Clon, though she was a Huguenot. Meanwhile I had a fright. The lanthorn, swinging in the sergeant's hand, and now throwing its smoky light on the stone seat, now on the rough wall above it, showed me something else. On the seat, doubtless where Mademoiselle's hand had lain, as she sat in the dark, listening and watching, stood a pitcher of food. Beside her, in that place, it was damning evidence. I trembled lest the lieutenant's eye should fall upon it, lest the sergeant should see it; I thought what I could do to hide it; and then in a moment I forgot all about it. The lieutenant was speaking, and his voice was like doom. My throat grew dry as I listened. My tongue stuck to my mouth; I tried to look at Mademoiselle, but I could not.

"It is true, the captain is gone," he said stiffly. "But others are alive, and about one of them, a word with you,--by your leave, Mademoiselle. I have listened to a good deal of talk from this fine gentleman friend of yours. He has spent the last twenty-four hours saying, 'You shall!' and 'You shall not!' He came from you, and took a very high tone because we laid a little whip-lash about that dumb devil of yours. He called us brutes and beasts, and but for him I am not sure that my friend would not be alive. But when he said a few minutes ago that he was glad,--glad of it, damn him!--then I fixed it in my mind that I would be even with him. And I am going to be!"

"What do you mean?" Mademoiselle asked, wearily interrupting him. "If you think you can prejudice me against that gentleman--"

"That is precisely what I do think! And I am going to do it. And a little more than that!"

"You will be only wasting your breath!" she answered proudly.

"Wait! wait, Mademoiselle, until you have heard!" he said. "If ever a black-hearted scoundrel, a dastardly, sneaking spy, trod the earth, it is this fellow! This friend of yours! And I am going to expose him. Your own eyes and your own ears shall persuade you. Why, I would not eat, I would not drink, I would not sit down with him! I would not! I would rather be beholden to the meanest trooper in my squadron than to him! Ay, I would, so help me Heaven!" And the lieutenant, turning squarely on his heels, spat on the ground.

THE ARREST

So it had come! And come in such a fashion that I saw no way of escape. The sergeant was between us, and I could not strike him. And I found no words. A score of times I had thought with shrinking how I should reveal my secret to Mademoiselle, what I should say, and how she would take it. But in my mind it had always been a voluntary act, this disclosure. It had been always I who had unmasked myself, and she who listened--alone; and in this voluntariness and this privacy there had been something which seemed to take from the shame of anticipation. But here-- here was no voluntary act on my part, no privacy, nothing but shame. I stood mute, convicted, speechless--like the thing I was.

Yet if anything could have braced me, it was Mademoiselle's voice, when she answered him. "Go on, Monsieur," she said, with the perfect calmness of scorn. "You will have done the sooner."

"You do not believe me?" he replied hotly. "Then, I say, look at him! Look at him! If ever shame--"

"Monsieur!" she said abruptly--she did not look at me. "I am ashamed myself!"

"Why, his very name is not his own!" the lieutenant rejoined jerkily. "He is no Barthe at all. He is Berault the gambler, the duellist, the bully--"

Again she interrupted him. "I know it," she said coldly. "I know it all. And if you have nothing more to tell me, go, Monsieur. Go!" she continued, in a tone of infinite scorn. "Enough that you have earned my contempt as well as my abhorrence!"

He looked for a moment taken aback. Then, "Ay, but I have more!" he cried, his voice stubbornly triumphant. "I forgot that you would think little of that! I forgot that a swordsman has always the ladies' hearts. But I have more. Do you know, too, that he is in the Cardinal's pay? Do you know that he is here on the same errand which brings us here,--to arrest M. de

Cocheforêt? Do you know that while we go about the business openly and in soldier fashion, it is his part to worm himself into your confidence, to sneak into Madame's intimacy, to listen at your door, to follow your footsteps, to hang on your lips, to track you--track you until you betray yourselves and the man? Do you know this, and that all his sympathy is a lie, Mademoiselle? His help, so much bait to catch the secret? His aim, blood-money--blood-money? Why, morbleu!" the lieutenant continued, pointing his finger at me, and so carried away by passion, so lifted out of himself by wrath and indignation, that in spite of myself I shrank before him,--"you talk, lady, of contempt and abhorrence in the same breath with me! But what have you for him? What have you for him, the spy, the informer, the hired traitor? And if you doubt, if you want evidence, look at him. Only look at him, I say!"

And he might well say it! For I stood silent still; cowering and despairing, white with rage and hate. But Mademoiselle did not look. She gazed straight at the lieutenant. "Have you done?" she said.

"Done?" he stammered. Her words, her air, brought him to earth again. "Done? Yes, if you believe me."

"I do not," she answered proudly. "If that be all, be satisfied, Monsieur. I do not believe you."

"Then tell me," he retorted, after a moment of stunned surprise, "why, if he was not on our side, do you think we let him remain here? Why did we suffer him to stay in a suspected house bullying us, and taking your part from hour to hour?"

"He has a sword, Monsieur," she answered, with fine contempt.

"Mille diables!" he cried, snapping his fingers in a rage. "That for his sword! No. It was because he held the Cardinal's commission; because he had equal authority with us; because we had no choice."

"And that being so, Monsieur, why are you now betraying him?" she asked keenly.

He swore at that, feeling the stroke go home. "You must be mad," he said, glaring at her. "Mad, if you cannot see that the man is what I tell you he is. Look at him! Listen to him! Has he a word to say for himself?"

Still she did not look. "It is late," she replied, coldly and irrelevantly. "And I am not very well. If you have quite done, perhaps you will leave me, Monsieur."

"Mon Dieu!" he exclaimed, shrugging his shoulders; "you are mad! I have told you the truth, and you will not believe it. Well, on your head be it then, Mademoiselle. I have no more to say. But you will see."

He looked at her for a moment as if he thought that she might still give way; then he saluted her roughly, gave the word to the sergeant, turned, and went down the path. The sergeant went after him, the lanthorn swaying in his hand. We two were left alone in the gloom. The frogs were croaking in the pool; the house, the garden, the wood,--all lay quiet under the darkness, as on the night when I first came to the Château.

And would to Heaven I had never come! That was the cry in my heart. Would to Heaven I had never seen this woman, whose nobility and faith and singleness were a continual shame to me; a reproach, branding me every hour I stood in her presence, with all vile and hateful names. The man just gone, coarse, low-bred, brutal soldier as he was, man-flogger, and drilling-block, had yet found heart to feel my baseness, and words in which to denounce it. What, then, would she say when the truth some day came home to her? What shape should I take in her eyes then? How should I be remembered through all the years--then?

Then? But now? What was she thinking, now, as she stood, silent and absorbed, by the stone seat, a shadowy figure with face turned from me? Was she recalling the man's words, fitting them to the facts and the past, adding this and that circumstance? Was she, though she had rebuffed him in the body, collating, now he was gone, all he had said, and out of these scraps piecing together the damning truth? The thought tortured me. I could brook uncertainty no longer. I went nearer to her and touched her sleeve. "Mademoiselle," I said, in a voice which sounded hoarse and forced even in my own ears, "do you believe this of me?"

She started violently and turned. "Pardon, Monsieur," she answered. "I had forgotten that you were here. Do I believe--what?"

"What that man said of me," I muttered.

"That!" she exclaimed; and she stood a moment gazing at me in a strange fashion. "Do I believe what he said, Monsieur! But come, come," she continued, "and I will show you if I believe it. But not here."

She led the way on the instant into the house, going in through the parlour door, which stood half open. The room inside was pitch dark, but she took me fearlessly by the hand, and led me quickly through it, and along the passage, until we came to the cheerful lighted hall, where a great fire burned on the hearth. All traces of the soldiers' occupation had been swept away. But the room was empty.

She led me to the fire, and there, in the full light, no longer a shadowy creature, but red-lipped, brilliant, throbbing with life, she stood opposite me, her eyes shining, her colour high, her breast heaving. "Do I believe it?" she said. "I will tell you. M. de Cocheforêt's hiding-place is in the hut behind the fern-stack, two furlongs beyond the village, on the road to Auch. You know now what no one else knows, he and I and Madame excepted. You hold in your hands his life and my honour; and you know also, M. de Berault, whether I believed that tale."

"My God!" I cried. And I stood looking at her, until something of the horror in my eyes crept into hers, and she shuddered and stepped back.

"What is it? What is it?" she whispered, clasping her hands. And with all the colour gone from her cheeks she peered trembling into the corners and towards the door. "There is no one here. Is there any one--listening?"

I forced myself to speak, though I shook all over, like a man in an ague. "No, Mademoiselle, there is no one here," I muttered. And then I let my head fall on my breast, and I stood before her, the statue of despair. Had she felt a grain of suspicion, a grain of doubt, my bearing must have opened her eyes. But her mind was cast in so noble a mould, that having once thought ill of me and been converted, she could feel no doubt again. It was her nature to trust all in all. So, a little recovered from her fright, she stood looking at me in great wonder; and at last she had a thought.

"You are not well?" she said suddenly. "It is your old wound, Monsieur."

"Yes, Mademoiselle," I muttered faintly. "It is my old wound."

"I will call Clon!" she cried impetuously. And then, with a sob, "Ah! poor Clon! He is gone. But there is Louis. I will call him, and he will get you something."

She was gone from the room before I could stop her; and I was left leaning against the table, possessor at last of the great secret which I had come so far to win. Possessor of that secret, and able in a moment to open the door, and go out into the night, and make use of it--and yet the most unhappy of men. The sweat stood on my brow, my eyes wandered round the room; I even turned towards the door, with some mad thought of flight--flight from her, from the house, from everything. And God knows if I might not have chosen that course; for I still stood doubting, when on the door, that door, there came a sudden hurried knocking which jarred every nerve in my body. I started. I stood in the middle of the floor, gazing at the door, as at a ghost. Then glad of action, glad of anything that might relieve the tension of my feelings, I strode to it, and pulled it sharply open.

On the threshold, his flushed face lit up by the light behind me, stood one of the knaves I had brought with me to Auch. He had been running, and panted heavily, but he had kept his wits. He grasped my sleeve instantly. "Ah! Monsieur, the very man!" he cried, tugging at me. "Quick! come this instant, and you may yet be first. They have the secret. They have found Monsieur."

"Found whom?" I echoed. "M. de Cocheforêt?"

"No; but the place where he lies. It was found by accident. The lieutenant was gathering his men to go to it when I came away. If we are quick, we may be there first."

"But the place?" I said.

"I could not hear where it was," he answered bluntly. "We can hang on their skirts, and at the last moment strike in."

The pair of pistols I had taken from the shock-headed man lay on a chest by the door. I snatched them up, and my hat, and joined him without another word; and in a moment we were running down the garden. I looked back once before we passed the gate, and I saw the light streaming out through the door which I had left open; and I fancied that for an instant a figure darkened the gap. But the fancy only strengthened the one single iron purpose which had taken possession of me and all my thoughts. I must be first. I must anticipate the lieutenant, and make the arrest myself. I ran on only the faster.

We seemed to be across the meadow and in the wood in a moment. There, instead of keeping along the common path, I boldly singled out--my senses seemed preternaturally keen--the smaller track by which Clon had brought us, and ran unfaltering along it, avoiding logs and pitfalls as by instinct, and following all its turns and twists, until it brought us to the back of the inn, and we could hear the murmur of subdued voices in the village street, the sharp low words of command, and even the clink of weapons; and could see, above and between the houses, the dull glare of lanthorns and torches.

I grasped my man's arm and crouched down, listening. "Where is your mate?" I said, in his ear.

"With them," he muttered.

"Then come," I whispered, rising. "I have seen enough. Let us go."

But he caught me by the arm and detained me. "You don't know the way!" he hissed. "Steady, steady, Monsieur. You go too fast. They are just moving. Let us join them, and strike in when the time comes. We must let them guide us."

"Fool!" I said, shaking off his hand. "I tell you, I know where he is! I know where they are going. Come; lose not a moment, and we will pluck the fruit while they are on the road to it."

His only answer was an exclamation of surprise; at that moment the lights began to move. The lieutenant was starting. The moon was not yet up; the sky was grey and cloudy; to advance where we were was to step into a wall of blackness. But we had lost too much time already, and I did not hesitate. Bidding my companion follow me, and use his legs, I sprang through a low fence which rose before us, and stumbling blindly over some broken ground in the rear of the houses, came, with a fall or two, to a little watercourse with steep sides. Through this I plunged recklessly, and up the farther side, and, breathless and panting, gained the road just beyond the village, and fifty yards in advance of the lieutenant's troop.

They had only two lanthorns burning now, and we were beyond the circle of light these cast; while the steady tramp of so many footsteps covered the noise we made. We were unnoticed. In a twinkling we turned our backs, and as fast as we could ran down the road. Fortunately, they were thinking more of secrecy than speed, and in a minute we had doubled the distance between us; in two minutes their lights were mere sparks shining in the gloom behind us. We lost, at last, even the tramp of their feet. Then I began to look out and go more slowly; peering into the shadows on either side for the fern-stack.

On one hand the hill rose steeply; on the other it fell away to the stream. On neither side was close wood,--or my difficulties had been immensely increased,--but scattered oak-trees stood here and there among gorse and bracken. This helped me, and in a moment, on the upper side, I came upon the dense substance of the stack looming black against the lighter hill.

My heart beat fast, but it was no time for thought. Bidding the man in a whisper to follow me and be ready to back me up, I climbed the bank softly, and with a pistol in my hand, felt my way to the rear of the stack; thinking to find a hut there, set against the fern, and M. de Cocheforêt in it. But I found no hut. There was none; and all was so dark that it came upon me suddenly as I stood between the hill and the stack that I had undertaken a very difficult thing. The hut behind the fern-stack? But how far behind? How far from it? The dark slope stretched above us, infinite, immeasurable, shrouded in night. To begin to climb it in search of a tiny hut, probably well-hidden and hard to find in daylight, seemed a task as impossible as to meet with the needle in the hay! And now, while I stood, chilled and doubting, the steps of the troop in the road began to grow audible, began to come nearer.

"Well, M. le Capitaine?" the man beside me muttered--in wonder why I stood. "Which way? Or they will be before us yet."

I tried to think, to reason it out; to consider where the hut would be; while the wind sighed through the oaks, and here and there I could hear an acorn fall. But the thing pressed too close on me: my thoughts would not be hurried, and at last I said at a venture, "Up the hill! Straight from the stack."

He did not demur, and we plunged at the ascent, knee deep in bracken and furze, sweating at every pore with our exertions, and hearing the troop come every moment nearer on the road below. Doubtless they knew exactly whither to go! Forced to stop and take breath when we had scrambled up fifty yards or so, I saw their lanthorns shining like moving glow-worms; and could even hear the clink of steel. For all I could tell, the hut might be down there, and we two be moving from it! But it was too late to go back now; they were close to the fern-stack: and in despair I turned to the hill again. A dozen steps, and I stumbled. I rose and plunged on again; again I stumbled. Then I found that I was no longer ascending. I was treading level earth. And--was it water I saw before me, below me, a little in front of my feet, or some mirage of the sky?

Neither; and I gripped my fellow's arm, as he came abreast of me, and stopped him sharply. Below us, in the centre of a steep hollow, a pit in the hill-side, a light shone out through some aperture and quivered on the mist, like the pale lamp of a moorland hobgoblin. It made itself visible, displaying nothing else; a wisp of light in the bottom of a black bowl.

Yet my spirits rose with a great bound at sight of it, for I knew that I had stumbled on the place I sought. In the common run of things I should have weighed my next step carefully, and gone about it slowly. But here was no place for thought, nor room for delay, and I slid down the side of the hollow, and the moment my feet touched the bottom, sprang to the door of the little hut whence the light issued. A stone turned under my foot in my rush, and I fell on my knees on the threshold; but the fall only brought my face to a level with the startled eyes of the man who lay inside on a bed of fern. He had been reading. At the sound I made he dropped his book, and stretched out his hand for a weapon. But the muzzle of my pistol covered him before he could reach his; he was not in a posture from which he could spring, and at a sharp word from me he dropped his hand. The tigerish glare which had flickered for an instant in his eyes, gave place to a languid smile; and he shrugged his shoulders. "Eh, bien?" he said, with marvellous composure. "Taken at last! Well, I was tired of it."

"You are my prisoner, M. de Cocheforêt," I answered.

"It seems so," he said.

"Move a hand, and I kill you," I answered. "But you have still a choice."

"Truly?" he said, raising his eyebrows.

"Yes. My orders are to take you to Paris alive or dead. Give me your parole that you will make no attempt to escape, and you shall go thither at your ease and as a gentleman. Refuse, and I shall disarm and bind you, and you will go as a prisoner."

"What force have you?" he asked curtly. He had not moved. He still lay on his elbow, his cloak covering him, the little Marot in which he had been reading close to his hand. But his quick, black eyes, which looked the keener for the pallor and thinness of his face, roved ceaselessly over me, probed the darkness behind me, took note of everything.

"Enough to compel you, Monsieur," I replied sternly. "But that is not all. There are thirty dragoons coming up the hill to secure you, and they will make you no such offer. Surrender to me before they come and give me your parole, and I will do all for your comfort. Delay, and you will fall into their hands. There can be no escape."

"You will take my word," he said slowly.

"Give it, and you may keep your pistols, M. de Cocheforêt," I replied.

"Tell me at least that you are not alone."

"I am not alone."

"Then I give it," he said, with a sigh. "And for Heaven's sake get me something to eat and a bed. I am tired of this pig-sty--and this life Arnidieu! it is a fortnight since I slept between sheets."

"You shall sleep to-night in your own house if you please," I answered hurriedly. "But here they come. Be good enough to stay where you are a moment, and I will meet them."

I stepped out into the darkness, in the nick of time. The lieutenant, after posting his men round the hollow, had just slid down with a couple of sergeants to make the arrest. The place round the open door was pitch dark. He had not espied my knave, who had lodged himself in the deepest shadow of the hut; and when he saw me come out across the light, he took me for Cocheforêt. In a twinkling he thrust a pistol into my face, and cried triumphantly, "You are my prisoner!" At the same instant one of the sergeants raised a lanthorn and threw its light into my eyes.

"What folly is this?" I said savagely.

The lieutenant's jaw fell, and he stood for half a minute, paralyzed with astonishment. Less than an hour before he had left me at the Château. Thence he had come hither with the briefest delay; and yet he found me here before him! He swore fearfully, his face dark, his mustachios stiff with rage. "What is this? What is it?" he cried at last. "Where is the man?"

"What man?" I said.

"This Cocheforêt!" he roared, carried away by his passion. "Don't lie to me! He is here, and I will have him!"

"You will not. You are too late!" I said, watching him heedfully. "M. de Cocheforêt is here, but he has already surrendered to me, and he is my prisoner."

"Your prisoner?"

"Yes, my prisoner!" I answered facing the man with all the harshness I could muster. "I have arrested him by virtue of the Cardinal's special commission granted to me. And by virtue of the same I shall keep him!"

He glared at me for a moment in utter rage and perplexity. Then on a sudden I saw his face lighten. "It is a d--d ruse!" he shouted, brandishing his pistol like a madman. "It is a cheat and a fraud! And by G--d you have no commission! I see through it! I see through it all! You have come here, and you have hocussed us! You are of their side, and this is your last shift to save him!"

"What folly is this?" I exclaimed.

"No folly at all!" he answered, conviction in his tone. "You have played upon us! You have fooled us! But I see through it now! An hour ago I exposed you to that fine Madame at the house there, and I thought it a marvel that she did not believe me. I thought it a marvel that she did not see through you, when you stood there before her, confounded, tongue-tied, a rogue convicted! But I understand it now. She knew you! By----, she knew you! She was in the plot, and you were in the plot; and I, who thought I was opening her eyes, was the only one fooled! But it is my turn now. You have played a bold part, and a clever one, and I congratulate you! But," he continued, a sinister light in his little eyes, "it is at an end now, Monsieur! You took us in finely with your tale of Monseigneur, and his commission, and your commission, and the rest. But I am not to be blinded any longer, or bullied! You have arrested him, have you? You have arrested him! Well, by G--d, I shall arrest him, and I shall arrest you too!"

"You are mad!" I said, staggered as much by this new view of the matter as by his perfect conviction of its truth. "Mad, Lieutenant!"

"I was!" he snarled drily. "But I am sane now. I was mad when you imposed upon us; when you persuaded me that you were fooling the women to get the secret out of them, while all the time you were sheltering them, protecting them, aiding them, and hiding him--then I was mad! But not now. However, I ask your pardon, M. de Barthe, or M. de Berault, or whatever your name really is. I ask your pardon. I thought you the cleverest sneak and the dirtiest hound heaven ever made, or hell refused! I find that you were cleverer than I thought, and an honest traitor. Your pardon."

One of the men who stood about the rim of the bowl above us laughed. I looked at the lieutenant, and could willingly have killed him. "Mon Dieu!" I said, so furious in my turn that I could scarcely speak. "Do you say that I am an impostor--that I do not hold the Cardinal's commission?"

"I do say that!" he answered coolly. "And shall abide by it."

"And that I belong to the rebel party?"

"I do," he replied, in the same tone. "In fact," with a grin, "I say that you are an honest man on the wrong side, M. de Berault. And you say that you are a scoundrel on the right. The advantage, however, is with me, and I shall back my opinion by arresting you."

A ripple of coarse laughter ran round the hollow. The sergeant who held the lanthorn grinned, and a trooper at a distance called out of the darkness, "A bon chat bon rat!" This brought a fresh burst of laughter, while I stood speechless, confounded by the stubbornness, the crassness, the insolence, of the man. "You fool!" I cried at last, "you fool!" And then M. de Cocheforêt, who had come out of the hut, and taken his stand at my elbow, interrupted me.

"Pardon me one moment," he said airily, looking at the lieutenant, with raised eyebrows, and pointing to me with his thumb. "But I am puzzled between you. This gentleman's name? Is it de Berault or de Barthe?"

"I am M. de Berault," I said brusquely, answering for myself.

"Of Paris?"

"Yes, Monsieur, of Paris."

"You are not then the gentleman who has been honouring my poor house with his presence?"

"Oh, yes!" the lieutenant struck in, grinning. "He is that gentleman, too!"

"But I thought--I understood that that was M. de Barthe."

"I am M. de Barthe, also," I retorted impatiently. "What of that, Monsieur? It was my mother's name. I took it when I came down here."

"To--er, to arrest me, may I ask?"

"Yes," I answered doggedly. "To arrest you. What of that?"

"Nothing," he replied slowly and with a steady look at me, a look I could not meet. "Except that, had I known this before, M. de Berault, I should have thought long before I surrendered to you."

The lieutenant laughed, and I felt my cheek burn. But I affected to see nothing, and turned to him again. "Now, Monsieur," I said sternly, "are you satisfied?"

"No!" he answered point blank. "I am not. You two gentlemen may have rehearsed this pretty scene a dozen times. The only word it seems to me, is, Quick March, back to Quarters."

I found myself driven to play my last card—much against my will. "Not so," I said; "I have my commission."

"Produce it!" he replied brusquely.

"Do you think that I carry it with me?" I said, in scorn. "Do you think that when I came here, alone, and not with fifty dragoons at my back, I carried the Cardinal's seal in my pocket for the first lackey to find? But you shall have it. Where is that knave of mine?"

The words were scarcely out of my mouth before his ready hand thrust a paper into my fingers. I opened it slowly, glanced at it, and amid a pause of surprise gave it to the lieutenant. He looked for a moment confounded. He stared at it, with his jaw fallen. Then with a last instinct of suspicion he bade the sergeant hold up the lanthorn, and by its light proceeded to spell out the document.

"Umph!" he ejaculated, after a moment's silence; and he cast an ugly look at me. "I see." And he read it aloud.

"By these presents I command and empower Gilles de Berault, sieur de Berault, to seek for, hold, arrest, and deliver to the Governor of the Bastile the body of Henri de Cocheforêt, and to do all such acts and things as shall be necessary to effect such arrest and delivery, for which these shall be his warrant.

"(Signed)   RICHELIEU, Lieut.-Gen."

When he had done,—and he read the signature with a peculiar intonation,—some one said softly, "Vive le roi!" and there was a moment's silence. The sergeant lowered his lanthorn. "Is it enough?" I said hoarsely, glaring from face to face.

The lieutenant bowed stiffly. "For me?" he said. "Quite, Monsieur. I beg your pardon again. I find that my first impressions were the-correct ones. Sergeant, give the gentleman his paper." And turning his shoulder rudely, he tossed the commission towards the sergeant, who picked it up, and gave it to me, grinning.

I knew that the clown would not fight, and he had his men round him; and I had no choice but to swallow the insult. As I put the paper in my breast, with as much indifference as I could assume, he gave a sharp order.

The troopers began to form on the edge above, the men who had descended, to climb the bank. As the group behind him began to open and melt away, I caught sight of a white robe in the middle of it. The next moment, appearing with a suddenness which was like a blow on the cheek to me, Mademoiselle de Cocheforêt glided forward, and came towards me. She had a hood on her head, drawn low; and for a moment I could not see her face. I forgot her brother's presence at my elbow; from habit and impulse rather than calculation, I took a step forward to meet her---though my tongue cleaved to the roof of my mouth, and I was dumb and trembling.

But she recoiled with such a look of white hate, of staring, frozen-eyed loathing, that I stepped back as if she had indeed struck me. It did not need the words which accompanied the look, the "Do not touch me!" which she hissed at me as she drew her skirts together, to drive me to the farther edge of the hollow; there to stand with clenched teeth and nails driven into the flesh while she hung, sobbing tearless sobs, on her brother's neck.

THE ROAD TO PARIS

I remember hearing Marshal Bassompierre, who, of all men within my knowledge, had the widest experience, say that not dangers, but discomforts, prove a man, and show what he is; and that the worst sores in life are caused by crumpled rose-leaves and not by thorns.

I am inclined to agree with this. For I remember that when I came from my room on the morning after the arrest, and found hall and parlour and passage empty, and all the common rooms of the house deserted, and no meal laid, and when I divined anew from this discovery the feeling of the house towards me,--however natural and to be expected,--I felt as sharp a pang as when, the night before, I had had to face discovery and open rage and scorn. I stood in the silent, empty parlour, and looked round me with a sense of desolation; of something lost and gone, which I could not replace. The morning was grey and cloudy, the air sharp; a shower was falling. The rose-bushes at the window swayed in the wind, and where I could remember the hot sunshine lying on floor and table, the rain beat in and stained the boards. The main door flapped and creaked to and fro. I thought of other days and meals I had taken there, and of the scent of flowers, and I fled to the hall in despair.

But here, too, was no sign of life or company, no comfort, no attendance. The ashes of the logs, by whose blaze Mademoiselle had told me the secret, lay on the hearth white and cold; and now and then a drop of moisture, sliding down the great chimney, pattered among them. The great door stood open as if the house had no longer anything to guard. The only living thing to be seen was a hound which roamed about restlessly, now gazing at the empty hearth, now lying down with pricked ears and watchful eyes. Some leaves which had been blown in rustled in a corner.

I went out moodily into the garden, and wandered down one path, and up another, looking at the dripping woods and remembering things, until I

111

came to the stone seat. On it, against the wall, trickling with rain-drops, and with a dead leaf half filling its narrow neck, stood the pitcher of food. I thought how much had happened since Mademoiselle took her hand off it and the sergeant's lanthorn disclosed it to me. And sighing grimly, I went in again through the parlour door.

A woman was on her knees, kindling the belated fire. I stood a moment, looking at her doubtfully, wondering how she would bear herself, and what she would say to me: and then she turned, and I cried out her name in horror; for it was Madame!

She was very plainly dressed; her childish face was wan, and piteous with weeping. But either the night had worn out her passion and drained her tears, or this great exigency gave her temporary calmness; for she was perfectly composed. She shivered as her eyes met mine, and she blinked as if a light had been suddenly thrust before her. But she turned again to her task, without speaking.

"Madame! Madame!" I cried, in a frenzy of distress. "What is this?"

"The servants would not do it," she answered, in a low but steady voice. "You are still our guest, Monsieur, and it must be done."

"But--I cannot suffer it!" I cried, in misery. "Madame de Cocheforêt, I will--I would rather do it myself!"

She raised her hand, with a strange, patient expression on her face. "Hush, please," she said. "Hush! you trouble me."

The fire took light and blazed up as she spoke, and she rose slowly from it, and, with a lingering look at it, went out; leaving me to stand and stare and listen in the middle of the floor. Presently I heard her coming back along the passage, and she entered, bearing a tray with wine and meat and bread. She set it down on the table, and with the same wan face, trembling always on the verge of tears, she began to lay out the things. The glasses clinked pitifully against the plates as she handled them; the knives jarred with one another; and I stood by, trembling myself, and endured this strange, this awful penance.

She signed to me at last to sit down and eat; and she went herself, and stood in the garden doorway, with her back to me. I obeyed. I sat down; but though I had eaten nothing since the afternoon of the day before, and a little earlier had had appetite enough, I could not swallow. I fumbled with my knife, and munched and drank; and grew hot and angry at this farce; and then looked through the window at the dripping bushes, and the rain, and the distant sundial, and grew cold again.

Suddenly she turned round and came to my side. "You do not eat," she said.

I threw down my knife, and sprang up in a frenzy of passion. "Mon Dieu! Madame!" I cried. "Do you think I have no heart?"

And then in a moment I knew what I had done. In a moment she was on her knees on the floor, clasping my knees, pressing her wet cheeks to my rough clothes, crying to me for mercy--for life! life! life! his life! Oh, it was horrible! It was horrible to see her fair hair falling over my mud-stained boots, to see her slender little form convulsed with sobs, to feel that this was a woman, a gentlewoman, who thus abased herself at my feet.

"Oh, Madame! Madame!" I cried, in my agony. "I beg you to rise. Rise, or I must go! You will drive me out!"

"Grant me his life!" she moaned passionately. "Only his life! What had he done to you, that you should hunt him down? What had we done to you, that you should slay us? Ah, Sir, have mercy! Let him go, and we will pray for you; I and my sister will pray for you every morning and night of our lives."

I was in terror lest some one should come and see her lying there, and I stooped and tried to raise her. But she would not rise; she only sank the lower until her tender hands clasped my spurs, and I dared not move. Then I took a sudden resolution. "Listen then, Madame," I said, almost sternly, "if you will not rise. When you ask what you do, you forget how I stand, and how small my power is! You forget that were I to release your husband to-day, he would be seized within the hour by those who are still in the village, and who are watching every road--who have not ceased to suspect my movements and my intentions. You forget, I say, my circumstances--"

She cut me short on that word. She sprang abruptly to her feet and faced me. One moment, and I should have said something to the purpose. But at that word she was before me, white, breathless, dishevelled, struggling for speech. "Oh yes, yes," she panted eagerly, "I know! I understand!" And she thrust her hand into her bosom and plucked something out and gave it to me--forced it upon me into my hands. "I know! I know!" she said again. "Take it, and God reward you, Monsieur! We give it freely--freely and thankfully! And may God bless you!"

I stood and looked at her, and looked at it, and slowly froze. She had given me the packet--the packet I had restored to Mademoiselle, the parcel of jewels. I weighed it in my hands, and my heart grew hard again, for I knew that this was Mademoiselle's doing; that it was she who, mistrusting the effect of Madame's tears and prayers, had armed her with this last weapon--this dirty bribe, I flung it down on the table among the plates, all my pity changed to anger. "Madame," I cried ruthlessly, "you mistake me altogether. I have heard hard words enough in the last twenty-four hours, and I know what you think of me! But you have yet to learn that I have never turned traitor to the hand that employed me, nor sold my own side! When I do so for a treasure ten times the worth of that, may my hand rot off!"

She sank into a seat, with a moan of despair, and at that moment the door opened, and M. de Cocheforêt came in. Over his shoulder I had a glimpse of Mademoiselle's proud face, a little whiter to-day, with dark marks under the eyes, but still firm and cold. "What is this?" he said, frowning and stopping short as his eyes lighted on Madame.

"It is--that we start at eleven o'clock, Monsieur," I answered, bowing curtly. "Those, I fancy, are your property." And pointing to the jewels, I went out by the other door.

That I might not be present at their parting, I remained in the garden until the hour I had appointed was well passed; then without entering the house I went to the stable entrance. Here I found all ready, the two troopers (whose company I had requisitioned as far as Auch) already in the saddle, my own two knaves waiting with my sorrel and M. de Cocheforêt's chestnut. Another horse was being led up and down by Louis, and, alas, my heart winced at the sight. For it bore a lady's saddle, and I saw that we were to have company. Was it Madame who meant to come with us? or Mademoiselle? And how far? To Auch? or farther?

I suppose that they had set some kind of a watch on me; for, as I walked up, M. de Cocheforêt and his sister came out of the house,--he looking white, with bright eyes and a twitching in his cheek, though through all he affected a jaunty bearing; she wearing a black mask.

"Mademoiselle accompanies us?" I said formally.

"With your permission, Monsieur," he answered, with grim politeness. But I saw that he was choking with emotion. I guessed that he had just parted from his wife, and I turned away.

When we were all mounted, he looked at me. "Perhaps, as you have my parole, you will permit me to ride alone," he said, with a little hesitation, "and--"

"Without me!" I rejoined keenly. "Assuredly, so far as is possible." I directed the troopers to ride in front and keep out of ear-shot; my two men followed the prisoner at a like distance, with their carbines on their knees. Last of all I rode myself, with my eyes open and a pistol loose in my holster. M. de Cocheforêt, I saw, was inclined to sneer at so many precautions, and the mountain made of his request; but I had not done so much and come so far, I had not faced scorn and insults, to be cheated of my prize at last. Aware that until we were beyond Auch there must be hourly and pressing danger of a rescue, I was determined that he who would wrest my prisoner from me should pay dearly for it. Only pride, and, perhaps, in a degree also, appetite for a fight, had prevented me borrowing ten troopers instead of two.

We started, and I looked with a lingering eye and many memories at the little bridge, the narrow woodland path, the first roofs of the village; all now familiar, all seen for the last time. Up the brook a party of soldiers were dragging for the captain's body. A furlong farther on, a cottage, burned by some carelessness in the night, lay a heap of black ashes. Louis ran beside us, weeping; the last brown leaves fluttered down in showers. And between my eyes and all, the slow, steady rain fell and fell and fell. And so I left Cocheforêt.

Louis went with us to a point a mile beyond the village, and there stood and saw us go, cursing me furiously as I passed. Looking back when we had ridden on, I still saw him standing; and after a moment's hesitation I rode back to him. "Listen, fool," I said, cutting him short in the midst of his mowing and snarling, "and give this message to your mistress. Tell her from me that it will be with her husband as it was with M. de Regnier, when he fell into the hands of his enemy--no better and no worse."

"You want to kill her, too, I suppose?" he answered, glowering at me.

"No, fool! I want to save her!" I retorted wrathfully. "Tell her that, just that and no more, and you will see the result."

"I shall not," he said sullenly. "I shall not tell her. A message from you, indeed!" And he spat on the ground.

"Then on your head be it!" I answered solemnly. And I turned my horse's head and galloped fast after the others. For, in spite of his refusal, I felt sure that he would report what I had said--if it were only out of curiosity; and it would be strange if Madame did not understand the reference.

And so we began our journey; sadly, under dripping trees and a leaden sky. The country we had to traverse was the same I had trodden on the last day of my march southwards, but the passage of a month had changed the face of everything. Green dells, where springs welling out of the chalk had made of the leafy bottom a fairies' home, strewn with delicate ferns and hung with mosses--these were now swamps into which our horses sank to the fetlock. Sunny brows, whence I had viewed the champaign and traced my forward path, had become bare, windswept ridges. The beech woods, which had glowed with ruddy light, were naked now; mere black trunks and rigid arms pointing to heaven. An earthy smell filled the air; a hundred paces away a wall of mist closed the view. We plodded on sadly, up hill and down hill; now fording brooks already stained with flood-water, now crossing barren heaths.

But up hill or down hill, whatever the outlook, I was never permitted to forget that I was the jailer, the ogre, the villain; that I, riding behind in my loneliness, was the blight on all, the death-spot. True, I was behind the others; I escaped their eyes. But there was not a line of Mademoiselle's drooping figure that did not speak scorn to me, not a turn of her head that did not seem to say, "Oh God, that such a thing should breathe!"

I had only speech with her once during the day, and that was on the last ridge before we went down into the valley to climb up again to Auch. The rain had ceased; the sun, near its setting, shone faintly; and for a few moments we stood on the brow and looked southwards while we breathed the horses. The mist lay like a pall on all the country we had traversed; but beyond it and above it, gleaming pearl-like in the level rays, the line of the mountains stood up like a land of enchantment, soft, radiant, wonderful, or like one of those castles on the Hill of Glass of which the old romances tell us. I forgot, for an instant, how we were placed, and I cried to my neighbour that it was the fairest pageant I had ever seen.

She--it was Mademoiselle, and she had taken off her mask--cast one look at me; only one, but it conveyed disgust and loathing so unspeakable that scorn beside them would have been a gift. I reined in my horse as if she had struck me, and felt myself go first hot and then cold under her eyes. Then she looked another way.

I did not forget the lesson; after that I avoided her more sedulously than before. We lay that night at Auch, and I gave M. de Cocheforêt the utmost liberty; even permitting him to go out and return at his will. In the morning, believing that on the farther side of Auch we ran less risk of attack, I dismissed the two dragoons, and an hour after sunrise we set out again. The day was dry and cold, the weather more promising. I planned to go by way of Lectoure, crossing the Garonne at Agen; and I thought with roads continually improving as we moved northwards, we should be able to make good progress before night. My two men rode first; I came last by myself.

Our way lay for some hours down the valley of the Gers, under poplars and by long rows of willows; and presently the sun came out and warmed us. Unfortunately, the rain of the day before had swollen the brooks which crossed our path, and we more than once had a difficulty in fording them. Noon, therefore, found us little more than half-way to Lectoure, and I was growing each minute more impatient, when our road, which had for a little while left the river bank, dropped down to it again, and I saw before us another crossing, half ford, half slough. My men tried it gingerly, and gave back, and tried it again in another place and finally, just as Mademoiselle and Monsieur came up to them, floundered through and sprang slantwise up the farther bank.

The delay had been long enough to bring me, with no good will of my own, close up to the Cocheforêts. Mademoiselle's horse made a little business of the place; this delayed them still longer, and in the result, we entered the water almost together, and I crossed close on her heels. The bank on either side was steep; while crossing we could see neither before nor behind. At the moment, however, I thought nothing of this, nor of her delay, and I was following her quite at my leisure, when the sudden report of a carbine, a second report, and a yell of alarm in front, thrilled me through.

On the instant, while the sound was still in my ears, I saw it all. Like a hot iron piercing my brain, the truth flashed into my mind. We were attacked! We were attacked, and I was here helpless in this pit, this trap!

The loss of a second while I fumbled here, Mademoiselle's horse barring the way, might be fatal.

There was but one way. I turned my horse straight at the steep bank, and he breasted it. One moment he hung as if he must fall back. Then, with a snort of terror and a desperate bound, he topped it, and gained the level, trembling and snorting.

It was as I had guessed. Seventy paces away on the road lay one of my men. He had fallen, horse and man, and lay still. Near him, with his back against a bank, stood his fellow, on foot, pressed by four horsemen, and shouting. As my eye lighted on the scene, he let fly with a carbine and dropped one.

I snatched a pistol from my holster, cocked it, and seized my horse by the head--I might save the man yet. I shouted to encourage him, and in another second should have charged into the fight, when a sudden vicious blow, swift and unexpected, struck the pistol from my hand.

I made a snatch at it as it fell, but missed it; and before I could recover myself, Mademoiselle thrust her horse furiously against mine, and with her riding-whip, lashed the sorrel across the ears. As my horse reared madly up, I had a glimpse of her eyes flashing hate through her mask; of her hand again uplifted; the next moment, I was down in the road, ingloriously unhorsed, the sorrel was galloping away, and her horse, scared in its turn, was plunging unmanageably a score of paces from me.

I don't doubt that but for that she would have trampled on me. As it was, I was free to draw; and in a twinkling I was running towards the fighters. All I have described had happened in a few seconds. My man was still defending himself; the smoke of the carbine had scarcely risen. I sprang with a shout across a fallen tree that intervened; at the same moment, two of the men detached themselves, and rode to meet me. One, whom I took to be the leader, was masked. He came furiously at me, trying to ride me down; but I leaped aside nimbly, and evading him, rushed at the other, and scaring his horse, so that he dropped his point, cut him across the shoulder before he could guard himself. He plunged away, cursing, and trying to hold in his horse, and I turned to meet the masked man.

"You double-dyed villain!" he cried, riding al. me again. And this time he manœuvred his horse so skilfully that I was hard put to it to prevent him knocking me down; and could not with all my efforts reach him to hurt him. "Surrender, will you!" he continued, "you bloodhound!"

I wounded him slightly in the knee for answer; but before I could do more his companion came back, and the two set upon me with a will, slashing at my head so furiously and towering above me with so great an advantage that it was all I could do to guard myself. I was soon glad to fall back against the bank--as my man had done before me. In such a conflict my rapier would have been of little use, but fortunately I had armed myself before I left Paris with a cut-and-thrust sword for the road; and though my mastery of the weapon was not on a par with my rapier-play, I was able to fend off their cuts, and by an occasional prick keep the horses at a distance. Still they swore and cut at me, trying to wear me out; and it was trying work. A little delay, the least accident, might enable the other man to come to their help, or Mademoiselle, for all I knew, might shoot me with my own pistol; and I confess, I was unfeignedly glad when a lucky parade sent the masked man's sword flying across the road. He was no coward; for unarmed as he was, he pushed his horse at me, spurring it recklessly; but the animal, which I had several times touched, reared up instead and threw him at the very moment that I wounded his companion a second time in the arm, and made him give back.

This quite changed the scene. The man in the mask staggered to his feet, and felt stupidly for a pistol. But he could not find one, and was, I saw, in no state to use it if he had. He reeled helplessly to the bank, and leaned against it. He would give no further trouble. The man I had wounded was in scarcely better condition. He retreated before me for some paces, but then losing courage, he dropped his sword, and, wheeling round, cantered off down the road, clinging to his pommel. There remained only the fellow engaged with my man, and I turned to see how they were getting on. They were standing to take breath, so I ran towards them; but, seeing me coming, this rascal, too, whipped round his horse, and disappeared in the wood, and left us masters of the field. The first thing I did--and I remember it to this day with pleasure--was to plunge my hand into my pocket, take out half the money I had in the world, and press it on the man who had fought for me so stoutly, and who had certainly saved me from disaster. In my joy I could have kissed him! It was not only that I had escaped defeat by the skin of my teeth,--and his good sword,--but I knew, and thrilled with the knowledge, that the fight had altered the whole position. He was wounded in two places, and I had a scratch or two, and had lost my horse; and my other poor fellow was dead as a herring. But speaking for myself, I would have spent half the blood in my body to purchase the feeling with which I turned back to speak to M. de Cocheforêt and his sister. I had fought before them.

Mademoiselle had dismounted, and with her face averted and her mask pushed on one side, was openly weeping. Her brother, who had scrupulously kept his place by the ford from the beginning of the fight to the end, met me with raised eyebrows and a peculiar smile. "Acknowledge my virtue," he said airily. "I am here, M. de Berault--which is more than can be said of the two gentlemen who have just ridden off."

"Yes," I answered, with a touch of bitterness. "I wish they had not shot my poor man before they went."

He shrugged his shoulders. "They were my friends," he said. "You must not expect me to blame them. But that is not all."

"No," I said, wiping my sword. "There is this gentleman in the mask." And I turned to go towards him.

"M. de Berault!" There was something abrupt in the way in which Cocheforêt called my name after me.

I stood. "Pardon?" I said, turning.

"That gentleman?" he answered, hesitating, and looking at me doubtfully. "Have you considered--what will happen to him, if you give him up to the authorities?"

"Who is he?" I said sharply.

"That is rather a delicate question," he answered, frowning, and still looking at me fixedly.

"Not from me," I replied brutally, "since he is in my power. If he will take off his mask, I shall know better what I intend to do with him."

The stranger had lost his hat in his fall, and his fair hair, stained with dust, hung in curls on his shoulders. He was a tall man, of a slender, handsome presence, and though his dress was plain and almost rough, I espied a splendid jewel on his hand, and fancied I detected other signs of high quality. He still lay against the bank in a half-swooning condition, and seemed unconscious of my scrutiny. "Should I know him if he unmasked?" I said suddenly, a new idea in my head.

"You would," M. de Cocheforêt answered simply.

"And?"

"It would be bad for every one."

"Ho, ho!" I said softly, looking hard, first at my old prisoner, and then at my new one. "Then, what do you wish me to do?"

"Leave him here," M. de Cocheforêt answered glibly, his face flushed, the pulse in his cheek beating. I had known him for a man of perfect honour before, and trusted him. But this evident earnest anxiety on behalf of his friend touched me. Besides, I knew that I was treading on slippery ground; that it behoved me to be careful. "I will do it," I said, after a moment's reflection. "He will play me no tricks, I suppose? A letter of--"

"Mon Dieu, no! He will understand," Cocheforêt answered eagerly. "You will not repent it, I swear. Let us be going."

"Well,--but my horse?" I said, somewhat taken aback by this extreme haste.

"We shall overtake it," he replied urgently. "It will have kept to the road. Lectoure is no more than a league from here, and we can give orders there to have these two fetched in and buried."

I had nothing to gain by demurring, and so it was arranged. After that we did not linger. We picked up what we had dropped, M. de Cocheforêt mounted his sister, and within five minutes we were gone. Casting a glance back from the skirts of the wood, as we entered it, I fancied that I saw the masked man straighten himself and turn to look after us; but the leaves were beginning to intervene, the distance was great and perhaps cheated me. And yet I was not disinclined to think the unknown a little less severely injured and a trifle more observant than he seemed.

AT THE FINGER POST

Through all, it will have been noticed, Mademoiselle had not spoken to me, nor said one word, good or bad. She had played her part grimly; had taken her defeat in silence, if with tears; had tried neither prayer, nor defence, nor apology. And the fact that the fight was now over, the scene left behind, made no difference in her conduct--to my surprise and discomfiture. She kept her face averted from me; she rode as before; she affected to ignore my presence. I caught my horse feeding by the road-side, a furlong forward, and mounted, and fell into place behind the two, as in the morning. And just as we had plodded on then in silence, we plodded on now, while I wondered at the unfathomable ways of women, and knowing that I had borne myself well, marvelled that she could take part in such an incident and remain unchanged.

Yet it had made a change in her. Though her mask screened her well, it could not entirely hide her emotions, and by-and-bye I marked that her head drooped, that she rode sadly and listlessly, that the lines of her figure were altered. I noticed that she had flung away, or furtively dropped, her riding-whip, and I understood that to the old hatred of me were now added shame and vexation; shame that she had so lowered herself, even to save her brother, vexation that defeat had been her only reward.

Of this I saw a sign at Lectoure, where the inn had but one common room, and we must all dine in company. I secured for them a table by the fire, and leaving them standing by it, retired myself to a smaller one, near the door. There were no other guests, and this made the separation between us more marked. M. de Cocheforêt seemed to feel this. He shrugged his shoulders and looked at me with a smile half sad, half comical. But Mademoiselle was implacable. She had taken off her mask, and her face was like stone. Once, only once, during the meal I saw a change come over her. She coloured, I suppose at her thoughts, until her face flamed from brow to chin. I watched the blush spread and spread, and then she slowly and proudly turned her shoulder to me, and looked through the window at the shabby street.

I suppose that she and her brother had both built on this attempt, Which must have been arranged at Auch. For when we went on in the afternoon, I saw a more marked change. They rode now like people resigned to the worst. The grey realities of the brother's position, the dreary, hopeless future, began to hang like a mist before their eyes; began to tinge the landscape with sadness; robbed even the sunset of its colours. With each hour their spirits flagged and their speech became less frequent, until presently, when the light was nearly gone and the dusk was round us, the brother and sister rode hand in hand, silent, gloomy, one at least of them weeping. The cold shadow of the Cardinal, of Paris, of the scaffold, was beginning to make itself felt; was beginning to chill them. As the mountains which they had known all their lives sank and faded behind us, and we entered on the wide, low valley of the Garonne, their hopes sank and faded also--sank to the dead-level of despair. Surrounded by guards, a mark for curious glances, with pride for a companion, M. de Cocheforêt could doubtless have borne himself bravely; doubtless he would bear himself bravely still when the end came. But almost alone, moving forward through the grey evening to a prison, with so many measured days before him, and nothing to exhilarate or anger,--in this condition it was little wonder if he felt, and betrayed that he felt, the blood run slow in his veins; if he thought more of the weeping wife and ruined home, which he left behind him, than of the cause in which he had spent himself.

But God knows, they had no monopoly of gloom. I felt almost as sad myself. Long before sunset the flush of triumph, the heat of the battle, which had warmed my heart at noon, were gone; giving place to a chill dissatisfaction, a nausea, a despondency, such as I have known follow a long night at the tables. Hitherto there had been difficulties to be overcome, risks to be run, doubts about the end. Now the end was certain, and very near; so near that it filled all the prospect. One hour of triumph I might still have; I hugged the thought of it as a gambler hugs his last stake. I planned the place and time and mode, and tried to occupy myself wholly with it. But the price? Alas, that would intrude too, and more as the evening waned; so that as I passed this or that thing by the road, which I could recall passing on my journey south,--with thoughts so different, with plans that now seemed so very, very old,--I asked myself grimly if this were really I, if this were Gil de Berault, known as Zaton's premier joueur; or some Don Quichotte from Castile, tilting at windmills, and taking barbers' bowls for gold.

We reached Agen very late in the evening, after groping through a by-way near the river, set with holes and willow-stools and frog-spawns--a place no better than a slough. After it the great fire and the lights at the Blue Maid seemed like a glimpse of a new world, and in a twinkling put something of life and spirits into two at least of us. There was queer talk round the hearth here of doings in Paris,--of a stir against the Cardinal, with the Queen-mother at bottom, and of grounded expectations that something might this time come of it. But the landlord pooh-poohed the idea, and I more than agreed with him. Even M. de Cocheforêt, who was for a moment inclined to build on it, gave up hope when he heard that it came only by way of Montauban; whence, since its reduction the year before, all sorts of canards against the Cardinal were always on the wing.

"They kill him about once a month," our host said, with a grin. "Sometimes it is Monsieur who is to prove a match for him, sometimes César Monsieur--the Duke of Vendôme, you understand,--and sometimes the Queen-mother. But since M. de Chalais and the Marshal made a mess of it, and paid forfeit, I pin my faith to His Eminence--that is his new title, they tell me."

"Things are quiet round here?" I asked.

"Perfectly. Since the Languedoc business came to an end, all goes well," he answered.

Mademoiselle had retired on our arrival, so that her brother and I were for an hour or two thrown together. I left him at liberty to separate himself if he pleased, but he did not use the opportunity. A kind of comradeship, rendered piquant by our peculiar relations, had begun to spring up between us. He seemed to take pleasure in my company, more than once rallied me on my post of jailer, would ask humorously if he might do this or that, and once even inquired what I should do if he broke his parole.

"Or take it this way," he continued flippantly "Suppose I had stuck you in the back this evening, in that cursed swamp by the river, M. de Berault? What then? Pardieu! I am astonished at myself that I did not do it. I could have been in Montauban within twenty-four hours, and found fifty hiding-places, and no one the wiser."

"Except your sister," I said quietly.

He laughed and shrugged his shoulders. "Yes," he said, "I am afraid I must have put her out of the way too, to preserve my self-respect. You are right." And on that he fell into a reverie which held him for a few minutes. Then I found him looking at me with a kind of frank perplexity that invited question.

"What is it?" I said.

"You have fought a great many duels?"

"Yes," I said.

"Did you never strike a foul blow in one of them?"

"Never. Why do you ask?"

"Well,--I wanted to confirm an impression," he said. "To be frank, M.

de Berault, I seem to see in you two men."

"Two men?"

"Yes, two men," he answered. "One, the man who captured me; the other, the man who let my friend go free to-day."

"It surprised you that I let him go? That was prudence, M. de Cocheforêt," I replied, "nothing more. I am an old gambler--I know when the stakes are too high for me. The man who caught a lion in his wolf-pit had no great catch."

"No, that is true," he answered, smiling. "And yet--I find two men in your skin."

"I dare say that there are two in most men's skins," I answered, with a sigh, "but not always together. Sometimes one is there, and sometimes the other."

"How does the one like taking up the other's work?" he asked keenly.

I shrugged my shoulders. "That is as may be," I said. "You do not take an estate without the debts."

He did not answer for a moment, and I fancied that his thoughts had reverted to his own case. But on a sudden he looked at me again. "Will you answer me a question, M. de Berault?" he said, with a winning smile.

"Perhaps," I said.

"Then tell me--it is a tale that is, I am sure, worth the telling. What was it that, in a very evil hour for me, sent you in search of me?"

"The Cardinal," I answered.

"I did not ask who," he replied drily. "I asked, what. You had no grudge against me?"

"No."

"No knowledge of me?"

"No."

"Then what on earth induced you to do it? Heavens, man," he continued bluntly, rising and speaking with greater freedom than he had before used, "nature never intended you for a tip staff! What was it, then?"

I rose too. It was very late, and the room was empty, the fire low. "I will tell you--tomorrow!" I said. "I shall have something to say to you then, of which that will be part."

He looked at me in great astonishment; with a little suspicion, too. But I put him off, and called for a light, and by going at once to bed, cut short his questions.

Those who know the great south road to Agen, and how the vineyards rise in terraces north of the town, one level of red earth above another, green in summer, but in late autumn bare and stony, will remember a particular place where the road two leagues from the town runs up a long hill. At the top of the hill four ways meet; and there, plain to be seen against the sky is a finger-post, indicating which way leads to Bordeaux, and which to Montauban, and which to Perigueux.

This hill had impressed me on my journey down; perhaps, because I had from it my first view of the Garonne valley, and there felt myself on the verge of the south country where my mission lay. It had taken root in my memory; I had come to look upon its bare, bleak brow, with the finger-post and the four roads, as the first outpost of Paris, as the first sign of return to the old life.

Now for two days I had been looking forward to seeing it again. That long stretch of road would do admirably for something I had in my mind. That sign-post, with the roads pointing north, south, east, and west, could there be a better place for meetings and partings?

We came to the bottom of the ascent about an hour before noon--M. de Cocheforêt, Mademoiselle, and I. We had reversed the order of yesterday, and I rode ahead. They came after me at their leisure. At the foot of the hill, however, I stopped and, letting Mademoiselle pass on, detained M. de Cocheforêt by a gesture. "Pardon me, one moment," I said. "I want to ask a favour."

He looked at me somewhat fretfully, with a gleam of wildness in his eyes that betrayed how the iron was eating into his heart. He had started after breakfast as gaily as a bridegroom, but gradually he had sunk below himself; and now he had much ado to curb his impatience. The bonhomie of last night was quite gone. "Of me?" he said. "What is it?"

"I wish to have a few words with Mademoiselle--alone," I explained.

"Alone?" he answered, frowning.

"Yes," I replied, without blenching, though his face grew dark. "For the matter of that, you can be within call all the time, if you please. But I have a reason for wishing to ride a little way with her."

"To tell her something?"

"Yes."

"Then you can tell it to me," he retorted suspiciously. "Mademoiselle, I will answer for it, has no desire to--"

"See me, or speak to me!" I said, taking him up. "I can understand that. Yet I want to speak to her."

"Very well, you can speak to her before me," he answered rudely. "Let us ride on and join her." And he made a movement as if to do so.

"That will not do, M. de Cocheforêt," I said firmly, stopping him with my hand. "Let me beg you to be more complaisant. It is a small thing I ask; but I swear to you, if Mademoiselle does not grant it, she will repent it all her life."

He looked at me, his face growing darker and darker. "Fine words!" he said presently, with a sneer. "Yet I fancy I understand them." Then with a passionate oath he broke out in a fresh tone. "But I will not have it. I have not been blind, M. de Berault, and I understand. But I will not have it! I will have no such Judas bargain made. Pardieu! do you think I could suffer it and show my face again?"

"I don't know what you mean!" I said, restraining myself with difficulty. I could have struck the fool.

"But I know what you mean," he replied, in a tone of repressed rage. "You would have her sell herself: sell herself body and soul to you to save me! And you would have me stand by and see the thing done! Well, my answer is--never! though I go to the wheel! I will die a gentleman, if I have lived a fool!"

"I think you will do the one as certainly as you have done the other," I retorted, in my exasperation. And yet I admired him.

"Oh, I am not such a fool," he cried, scowling at me, "as you have perhaps thought. I have used my eyes."

"Then be good enough now to favour me with your ears," I answered drily. "And listen when I say that no such bargain has ever crossed my mind. You were kind enough to think well of me last night, M. de Cocheforêt. Why should the mention of Mademoiselle in a moment change your opinion? I wish simply to speak to her. I have nothing to ask from her; neither favour nor anything else. And what I say she will doubtless tell you afterwards. Ciel, man!" I continued angrily, "what harm can I do to her, in the road, in your sight?"

He looked at me sullenly, his face still flushed, his eyes suspicious. "What do you want to say to her?" he asked jealously. He was quite unlike himself. His airy nonchalance, his careless gaiety, were gone.

"You know what I do not want to say to her, M. de Cocheforêt," I answered. "That should be enough."

He glowered at me for a moment, still ill content. Then, without a word, he made me a gesture to go to her.

She had halted a score of paces away, wondering doubtless what was on foot. I rode towards her. She wore her mask, so that I lost the expression of her face as I approached, but the manner in which she turned her horse's head uncompromisingly towards her brother, and looked past me--as if I were merely a log in the road--was full of meaning. I felt the ground suddenly cut from under me. I saluted her, trembling. "Mademoiselle," I said, "will you grant me the privilege of your company for a few minutes, as we ride."

"To what purpose, Sir?" she answered, in the coldest voice in which I think a woman ever spoke to a man.

"That I may explain to you a great many things you do not understand," I murmured.

"I prefer to be in the dark," she replied. And her manner said more than her words.

"But, Mademoiselle," I pleaded,--I would not be discouraged,--"you told me one day that you would never judge me hastily again."

"Facts judge you, not I, Sir," she answered icily. "I am not sufficiently on a level with you to be able to judge you--I thank God."

I shivered though the sun was on me, and the hollow where we stood was warm. "Still--once before you thought the same!" I exclaimed. "Afterwards you found that you had been wrong. It may be so again, Mademoiselle."

"Impossible," she said.

That stung me. "No!" I said fiercely. "It is not impossible. It is you who are impossible! It is you who are heartless, Mademoiselle. I have done much, very much, in the last three days to make things lighter for you. I ask you now to do something for me which can cost you nothing."

"Nothing?" she answered slowly; and her scornful voice cut me as if it had been a knife. "Do you think, Monsieur, it costs me nothing to lose my self-respect, as I do with every word I speak to you? Do you think it costs me nothing to be here, where I feel every look you cast on me an insult, every breath I take in your presence a contamination. Nothing, Monsieur?" She laughed in bitter irony. "Oh, be sure, something! But something which I despair of making clear to you."

I sat for a moment in my saddle, shaken and quivering with pain. It had been one thing to feel that she hated and scorned me, to know that the trust and confidence which she had begun to place in me were changed to loathing. It was another to listen to her hard, pitiless words, to change colour under the lash of her gibing tongue. For a moment I could not find voice to answer her. Then I pointed to M. de Cocheforêt. "Do you love him?" I said, hoarsely, roughly. The gibing tone had passed from her voice to mine.

She did not answer.

"Because, if you do," I continued, "you will let me tell my tale. Say no but once more, Mademoiselle,--I am only human,--and I go. And you will repent it all your life."

I had done better had I taken that tone from the beginning. She winced, her head drooped, she seemed to grow smaller. All in a moment, as it were, her pride collapsed. "I will hear you," she answered feebly.

"Then we will ride on, if you please," I said, keeping the advantage I had gained. "You need not fear. Your brother will follow."

I caught hold of her rein and turned her horse, and she suffered it without demur. In a moment we were pacing side by side, the long, straight road before us. At the end where it topped the hill, I could see the finger-post,--two faint black lines against the sky. When we reached that, involuntarily I checked my horse and made it move more slowly.

"Well, Sir," she said impatiently. And her figure shook as if with cold.

"It is a tale I desire to tell you, Mademoiselle," I answered, speaking with effort. "Perhaps I may seem to begin a long way off, but before I end, I promise to interest you. Two months ago there was living in Paris a man, perhaps a bad man, at any rate, by common report, a hard man."

She turned to me suddenly, her eyes gleaming through her mask. "Oh, Monsieur, spare me this!" she said, quietly scornful. "I will take it for granted."

"Very well," I replied steadfastly. "Good or bad, this man, one day, in defiance of the Cardinal's edict against duelling, fought with a young Englishman behind St. Jacques Church. The Englishman had influence, the person of whom I speak had none, and an indifferent name; he was arrested, thrown into the Châtelet, cast for death, left for days to face death. At the last an offer was made to him. If he would seek out and deliver up another man, an outlaw with a price upon his head, he should himself go free."

I paused and drew a deep breath. Then I continued, looking not at her, but into the distance: "Mademoiselle, it seems easy now to say what course he should have chosen. It seems hard now to find excuses for him. But there was one thing which I plead for him. The task he was asked to undertake was a dangerous one. He risked, he knew he must risk, and the event proved him right, his life against the life of this unknown man. And-- one thing more--there was time before him. The outlaw might be taken by another, might be killed, might die, might--. But there, Mademoiselle, we know what answer this person made. He took the baser course, and on his honour, on his parole, with money supplied to him, went free,--free on the condition that he delivered up this other man."

I paused again, but I did not dare to look at her, and after a moment of silence I resumed. "Some portion of the second half of this story you know, Mademoiselle; but not all. Suffice it that this man came down to a remote village, and there at a risk, but Heaven knows, basely enough, found his way into his victim's home. Once there, his heart began to fail him. Had he found the house garrisoned by men, he might have pressed on to his end with little remorse. But he found there only two helpless, loyal women; and I say again that from the first hour of his entrance he sickened of the work he had in hand. Still he pursued it. He had given his word, and if there was one tradition of his race which this man had never broken, it was that of fidelity to his side; to the man that paid him. But he pursued it with only half his mind, in great misery sometimes, if you will believe me, in agonies of shame. Gradually, however, almost against his will, the drama worked itself out before him, until he needed only one thing."

I looked at Mademoiselle. But her head was averted; I could gather nothing from the outlines of her form. And I went on. "Do not misunderstand me," I said, in a lower voice. "Do not misunderstand what I am going to say next. This is no love story, and can have no ending such as romancers love to set to their tales. But I am bound to mention, Mademoiselle, that this man, who had lived about inns and eating-houses, and at the gaming-tables almost all his days, met here for the first time for years a good woman; and learned by the light of her loyalty and devotion to see what his life had been, and what was the real nature of the work he was doing. I think,--nay, I know--that it added a hundredfold to his misery, that when he learned at last the secret he had come to surprise, he learned it from her lips, and in such a way that had he felt no shame, hell could have been no place for him. But in one thing she misjudged him. She thought, and had reason to think, that the moment he knew her secret he went out, not even closing the door, and used it. But the truth was that, while her words were still in his ears, news came to him that others had the secret; and had he not gone out on the instant, and done what he did, and forestalled them, M. de Cocheforêt would have been taken, but by others."

Mademoiselle broke her long silence so suddenly that her horse sprang forward. "Would to Heaven he had!" she wailed.

"Been taken by others?" I exclaimed, startled out of my false composure.

"Oh, yes, yes!" she answered passionately. "Why did you not tell me? Why did you not confess to me even then? I--oh, no more! No more!" she continued, in a piteous voice. "I have heard enough. You are racking my heart, M. de Berault. Some day I will ask God to give me strength to forgive you."

"But you have not heard me out," I replied.

"I want to hear no more," she answered, in a voice she vainly strove to render steady. "To what end? Can I say more than I have said? Did you think I could forgive you now--with him behind us going to his death? Oh, no, no!" she continued. "Leave me! I implore you to leave me. I am not well."

She drooped over her horse's neck as she spoke and began to weep so passionately that the tears ran down her cheeks under her mask, and fell and sparkled like dew on the mane before her; while her sobs shook her so painfully that I thought she must fall. I stretched out my hand instinctively to give her help; but she shrank from me. "No!" she gasped, between her sobs. "Do not touch me. There is too much between us."

"Yet there must be one thing more between us," I answered firmly. "You must listen to me a little longer, whether you will or no, Mademoiselle, for the love you bear to your brother. There is one course still open to me by which I may redeem my honour; it has been in my mind for some time back to take that course. To-day, I am thankful to say, I can take it cheerfully, if not without regret; with a steadfast heart, if with no light one. Mademoiselle," I continued earnestly, feeling none of the triumph, none of the vanity, I had foreseen, but only joy in the joy I could give her, "I thank God that it is still in my power to undo what I have done; that it is still in my power to go back to him who sent me, and telling him that I have changed my mind and will bear my own burdens, to pay the penalty."

We were within a hundred paces of the brow of the hill and the finger-post now. She cried out wildly that she did not understand. "What is it you have just said?" she murmured. "I cannot hear." And she began to fumble with the ribbon of her mask.

"Only this, Mademoiselle," I answered gently. "I give back to your brother his word and his parole. From this moment he is free to go whither he pleases. You shall tell him so from me. Here, where we stand, four roads meet. That to the right goes to Montauban, where you have doubtless friends, and can lie hid for a time; or that to the left leads to Bordeaux, where you can take ship if you please. And in a word Mademoiselle," I continued, ending a little feebly, "I hope that your troubles are now over."

She turned her face to me--we had both come to a standstill--and plucked at the fastenings of her mask. But her trembling fingers had knotted the string, and in a moment she dropped her hands with a cry of despair. "And you? You?" she said, in a voice so changed I should not have known it for hers. "What will you do? I do not understand. This mask! I cannot hear."

"There is a third road," I answered. "It leads to Paris. That is my road, Mademoiselle. We part here."

"But why? Why?" she cried wildly.

"Because from to-day I would fain begin to be honourable," I answered, in a low voice. "Because I dare not be generous at another's cost I must go back to the Châtelet."

She tried feverishly to raise her mask with her hand. "I am--not well," she stammered. "I cannot breathe."

She swayed so violently in her saddle as she spoke, that I sprang down, and running round her horse's head, was just in time to catch her as she fell. She was not quite unconscious then, for, as I supported her, she murmured, "Leave me! Leave me! I am not worthy that you should touch me."

Those words made me happy. I carried her to the bank, my heart on fire, and laid her against it just as M. de Cocheforêt rode up. He sprang from his horse, his eyes blazing with anger. "What is this?" he cried harshly. "What have you been saying to her, man?"

"She will tell you," I answered drily, my composure returning under his eye,--"amongst other things, that you are free. From this moment, M. de Cocheforêt, I give you back your parole, and I take my own honour. Farewell."

He cried out something as I mounted, but I did not stay to hear or answer. I dashed the spurs into my horse, and rode away past the crossroads, past the finger-post; away with the level upland stretching before me, dry, bare, almost treeless--and behind me all I loved. Once, when I had gone a hundred yards, I looked back and saw him standing upright against the sky, staring after me across her body. And again I looked back. This time I saw only the slender wooden cross, and below it a dark blurred mass.

ST. MARTIN'S EVE

It was late evening on the last day but one of November, when I rode into Paris through the Orleans gate. The wind was in the northeast, and a great cloud of vapour hung in the eye of an angry sunset. The air seemed to be full of wood smoke, the kennels reeked, my gorge rose at the city's smell; and with all my heart I envied the man who had gone out of it by the same gate nearly two months before, with his face to the south, and the prospect of riding day after day across heath and moor and pasture. At least he had had some weeks of life before him, and freedom, and the open air, and hope and uncertainty, while I came back under doom; and in the pall of smoke that hung over the huddle of innumerable roofs, saw a gloomy shadowing of my own fate.

For make no mistake. A man in middle life does not strip himself of the worldly habit with which experience has clothed him, does not run counter to all the cynical saws and instances by which he has governed his course so long, without shiverings and doubts and horrible misgivings and struggles of heart. At least a dozen times between the Loire and Paris, I asked myself what honour was; and what good it would do me when I lay rotting and forgotten; if I was not a fool following a Jack-o'-lanthorn; and whether, of all the men in the world, the relentless man to whom I was returning, would not be the first to gibe at my folly.

However, shame kept me straight; shame and the memory of Mademoiselle's looks and words. I dared not be false to her again; I could not, after speaking so loftily, fall so low. And therefore--though not without many a secret struggle and quaking--I came, on this last evening but one of November, to the Orleans gate, and rode slowly and sadly through the streets by the Luxembourg, on my way to the Pont au Change.

The struggle had sapped my last strength, however; and with the first whiff of the gutters, the first rush of barefooted gamins under my horse's hoofs, the first babel of street cries, the first breath, in a word, of Paris, there came a new temptation--to go for one last night to Zaton's to see the tables again and the faces of surprise; to be, for an hour or two, the old Berault. That could be no breach of honour; for in any case I could not reach the Cardinal before tomorrow. And it could do no harm. It could make no change in anything. It would not have been a thing worth struggling about--only I had in my inmost heart suspicions that the stoutest resolutions might lose their force in that atmosphere; that even such a talisman as the memory of a woman's looks and words might lose its virtue there.

Still I think I should have succumbed in the end, if I had not received at the corner of the Luxembourg a shock which sobered me effectually. As I passed the gates, a coach followed by two outriders swept out of the palace courtyard; it was going at a great pace, and I reined my jaded horse on one side to give it room. As it whirled by me, one of the leather curtains flapped back, and I saw for a second, by the waning light,--the nearer wheels were no more than two feet from my boot,--a face inside.

A face, and no more, and that only for a second! But it froze me. It was Richelieu's, the Cardinal's; but not as I had been wont to see it, keen, cold, acute, with intellect and indomitable will in every feature. This face was distorted with rage and impatience; with the fever of haste and the fear of death. The eyes burned under the pale brow, the mustachios bristled, the teeth showed through the beard; I could fancy the man crying "Faster! Faster!" and gnawing his nails in the impatience of passion; and I shrank back as if I had been struck. The next moment the galloping outriders splashed me, the coach was a hundred paces ahead, and I was left chilled and wondering, foreseeing the worst, and no longer in any mood for the gaming-table.

Such a revelation of such a man was enough to appall me. Conscience cried out that he must have heard that Cocheforêt had escaped, and through me! But I dismissed the idea as soon as formed.

In the vast meshes of the Cardinal's schemes, Cocheforêt could be only a small fish; and to account for the face in the coach I needed a cataclysm, a catastrophe, a misfortune, as far above ordinary mishaps, as this man's intellect rose above the common run of minds.

It was almost dark when I crossed the bridges, and crept despondently to the Rue Savonnerie. After stabling my horse, I took my bag and holsters, and climbing the stairs to my old landlord's,--the place seemed to have grown strangely mean and small and ill-smelling in my absence,--I knocked at the door. It was opened by the little tailor himself, who threw up his arms at the sight of me. "By St. Genevieve!" he said. "If it is not M. de Berault!"

"No other," I said. It touched me a little, after my lonely journey, to find him so glad to see me--though I had never done him a greater benefit than sometimes to unbend with him and borrow his money. "You look surprised, little man!" I continued, as he made way for me to enter. "I'll be sworn you have been pawning my goods and letting my room, you knave!"

"Never, your excellency!" he answered, beaming on me. "On the contrary, I have been expecting you."

"How?" I said. "To-day?"

"To-day or to-morrow," he answered, following me in and closing the door. "The first thing I said, when I heard the news this morning, was, Now we shall have M. de Berault back again. Your excellency will pardon the children," he continued, as I took the old seat on the three-legged stool before the hearth. "The night is cold, and there is no fire in your room."

While he ran to and fro with my cloak and bags, little Gil, to whom I had stood at St. Sulpice's--borrowing ten crowns the same day, I remember--came shyly to play with my sword-hilt "So you expected me back when you heard the news, Frison, did you?" I said, taking the lad on my knee.

"To be sure, your excellency," he answered, peeping into the black pot before he lifted it to the hook.

"Very good. Then, now, let us hear what the news was," I said drily.

"Of the Cardinal, M. de Berault."

"Ah? And what?"

He looked at me, holding the heavy pot suspended in his hands. "You have not heard?" he exclaimed, his jaw falling.

"Not a tittle. Tell it me, my good fellow."

"You have not heard that His Eminence is disgraced?"

I stared at him. "Not a word," I said.

He set down the pot. "Your excellency must have made a very long journey indeed, then," he said, with conviction. "For it has been in the air a week or more, and I thought it had brought you back. A week? A month, I dare say. They whisper that it is the old Queen's doing. At any rate, it is certain that they have cancelled his commissions and displaced his officers. There are rumours of immediate peace with Spain. His enemies are lifting up their heads, and I hear that he has relays of horses set all the way to the coast, that he may fly at any moment For what I know he may be gone already."

"But, man," I said--"the King! You forget the King. Let the Cardinal once pipe to him, and he will dance. And they will dance, too!" I added grimly.

"Yes," Frison answered eagerly. "True, your excellency, but the King will not see him. Three times to-day, as I am told, the Cardinal has driven to the Luxembourg, and stood like any common man in the ante-chamber, so that I hear it was pitiful to see him. But His Majesty would not admit him. And when he went away the last time, I am told that his face was like death!

Well, he was a great man, and we may be worse ruled, M. de Berault, saving your presence. If the nobles did not like him, he was good to the traders, and the bourgeoisie, and equal to all."

"Silence, man! Silence, and let me think," I said, much excited. And while he bustled to and fro, getting my supper, and the firelight played about the snug, sorry little room, and the child toyed with his plaything, I fell to digesting this great news, and pondering how I stood now and what I ought to do. At first sight, I know, it seemed that I had nothing to do but sit still. In a few hours the man who held my bond would be powerless, and I should be free. In a few hours I might smile at him. To all appearance, the dice had fallen well for me. I had done a great thing, run a great risk, won a woman's love, and after all was not to pay the penalty!

But a word which fell from Frison as he fluttered round me, pouring out the broth, and cutting the bread, dropped into my mind and spoiled my satisfaction. "Yes, your excellency," he exclaimed, confirming something he had said before, and which I had missed, "and I am told that the last time he came into the gallery, there was not a man of all the scores who attended his levée last Monday would speak to him. They fell off like rats,--just like rats,--until he was left standing all alone. And I have seen him!" Frison lifted up his eyes and his hands and drew in his breath. "Ah, I have seen the King look shabby beside him! And his eye! I would not like to meet it now."

"Pish!" I growled. "Some one has fooled you. Men are wiser than that."

"So? Well, your excellency understands. But--there are no cats on a cold hearth."

I told him again that he was a fool. But withal I felt uncomfortable. This was a great man if ever a great man lived, and they were all leaving him; and I--well, I had no cause to love him. But I had taken his money, I had accepted his commission, and I had betrayed him. Those three things being so, if he fell before I could--with the best will in the world--set myself right with him, so much the better for me. That was my gain, the fortune of war. But if I lay hid, and took time for my ally, and being here while he stood still,--though tottering,--waited until he fell, what of my honour then? What of the grand words I had said to Mademoiselle at Agen? I should be like the recreant in the old romance, who, lying in the ditch while the battle raged, came out afterwards and boasted of his courage. And yet the flesh was weak. A day, twenty-four hours, two days, might make the difference between life and death. At last I settled what I would do. At noon the next day, the time at which I should have presented myself, if I had not heard this news, at that time I would still present myself. Not earlier; I owed myself the chance. Not later; that was due to him.

Having so settled it, I thought to rest in peace. But with the first light I was awake; and it was all I could do to keep myself quiet until I heard

Frison stirring. I called to him then to know if there was any news, and lay waiting and listening while he went down to the street to learn. It seemed an endless time before he came back; an age, after he came back, before he spoke.

"Well, he has not set off?" I cried at last, unable to control my eagerness.

Of course he had not. At nine o'clock I sent Frison out again; and at ten, and at eleven--always with the same result. I was like a man waiting, and looking, and, above all, listening for a reprieve, and as sick as any craven. But when he came back at eleven, I gave up hope, and dressed myself carefully. I suppose I still had an odd look, however; for Frison stopped me at the door and asked me, with evident alarm, whither I was going.

I put the little man aside gently. "To the tables," I said. "To make a big throw, my friend."

It was a fine morning; sunny, keen, pleasant. Even the streets smelled fresh. But I scarcely noticed it. All my thoughts were where I was going. It seemed but a step from my threshold to the Hotel Richelieu. I was no sooner gone from the one than I found myself at the other. As on the memorable evening, when I had crossed the street in a drizzling rain, and looked that way with foreboding, there were two or three guards in the Cardinal's livery, loitering before the gates. But this was not all. Coming nearer, I found the opposite pavement under the Louvre thronged with people; not moving about their business, but standing all silent, all looking across furtively, all with the air of persons who wished to be thought passing by. Their silence and their keen looks had in some way an air of menace. Looking back after I had turned in towards the gates, I found them devouring me with their eyes.

Certainly they had little else to look at. In the courtyard, where some mornings when the court was in Paris I had seen a score of coaches waiting and thrice as many servants, were now emptiness and sunshine and stillness. The officer, who stood twisting his mustachios, on guard, looked at me in wonder as I passed. The lackeys lounging in the portico, and all too much taken up with whispering to make a pretence of being of service, grinned at my appearance. But that which happened when I had mounted the stairs, and come to the door of the ante-chamber, outdid all. The man on guard there would have opened the door; but when I went to take advantage of the offer, and enter, a major-domo, who was standing near, muttering with two or three of his kind, hastened forward and stopped me.

"Your business, Monsieur, if you please?" he said inquisitively. And I wondered why the others looked at me so strangely.

"I am M. de Berault," I answered sharply. "I have the entrée."

He bowed politely enough. "Yes, M. de Berault, I have the honour to know your face," he said. "But pardon me. Have you business with His Eminence?"

"I have the common business," I answered bluntly, "by which many of us live, sirrah!--to wait on him."

"But--by appointment, Monsieur?" he persisted.

"No," I said, astonished. "It is the usual hour. For the matter of that, however, I have business with him."

The man looked at me for a moment, in apparent embarrassment. Then he stood reluctantly aside, and signed to the door-keeper to open the door. I passed in, uncovering, with an assured face, ready to meet all eyes. Then in a moment, on the threshold, the mystery was explained.

The room was empty.

ST. MARTIN'S SUMMER

Yes, at the great Cardinal's levée I was the only client. I stared round the room, a long narrow gallery, through which it was his custom to walk every morning, after receiving his more important visitors. I stared, I say, round this room, in a state of stupefaction. The seats against either wall were empty, the recesses of the windows empty too. The hat, sculptured and painted here and there, the staring R, the blazoned arms, looked down on a vacant floor. Only, on a little stool by the main door, sat a quiet-faced man in black, who read, or pretended to read, in a little book, and never looked up. One of those men, blind, deaf, secretive, who fatten in the shadow of the great.

At length, while I stood confounded and full of shamed thought,--for I had seen the ante-chamber of Richelieu's old hotel so crowded that he could not walk through it,--this man closed his book, rose, and came noiselessly towards me. "M. de Berault?" he said.

"Yes," I answered.

"His Eminence awaits you. Be good enough to follow me."

I did so, in a deeper stupor than before. For how could the Cardinal know that I was here? How could he have known when he gave the order? But I had short time to think of these things. We passed through two rooms, in one of which some secretaries were writing; we stopped at a third door. Over all brooded a silence which could be felt. The usher knocked, opened, and with his finger on his lip, pushed aside a curtain, and signed to me to enter. I did so, and found myself standing behind a screen.

"Is that M. de Berault?" asked a thin, high-pitched voice.

"Yes, Monseigneur," I answered, trembling.

"Then come, my friend, and talk to me."

I went round the screen; and I know not how it was, the watching crowd outside, the vacant antechamber in which I had stood, the stillness,--

all seemed concentrated here, and gave to the man I saw before me, a dignity which he had never possessed for me when the world passed through his doors, and the proudest fawned on him for a smile. He sat in a great chair on the farther side of the hearth, a little red skull-cap on his head, his fine hands lying motionless in his lap. The collar of lawn which fell over his red cape was quite plain, but the skirts of his red robe were covered with rich lace, and the order of the Holy Ghost shone on his breast. Among the multitudinous papers on the great table near him I saw a sword and pistols lying; and some tapestry that covered a little table behind him failed to hide a pair of spurred riding-boots. But he--in spite of these signs of trouble--looked towards me as I advanced, with a face mild and almost benign; a face in which I strove in vain to find traces of last night's passion. So that it flashed across me that if this man really stood--and afterwards I knew he did--on the thin razor-edge between life and death, between the supreme of earthly power, lord of France, and arbiter of Europe, and the nothingness of the clod, he justified his fame. He gave weaker natures no room for triumph.

The thought was no sooner entertained than it was gone. "And so you are back at last, M. de Berault?" he said, gently. "I have been expecting to see you since nine this morning."

"Your Eminence knew then--" I muttered.

"That you returned to Paris by the Orleans gate last evening, alone?" He fitted together the ends of his fingers, and looked at me over them with inscrutable eyes. "Yes, I knew all that last night. And now of your mission? You have been faithful, and diligent, I am sure. Where is he?"

I stared at him, and was dumb. Somehow the strange things I had seen since I left my lodging, the surprises I had found awaiting me here, had driven my own fortunes, my own peril, out of my head, until this moment. Now, at his question, all returned with a rush. My heart heaved suddenly in my breast. I strove for a savour of the old hardihood; but for the moment I could not find a word.

"Well?" he said lightly, a faint smile lifting his mustache. "You do not speak. You left Auch with him on the twenty-fourth, M. de Berault. So much I know. And you reached Paris without him last night. He has not given you the slip?" with sudden animation.

"No, Monseigneur," I muttered.

"Ha! That is good," he answered, sinking back again in his chair. "For the moment--but I knew I could depend on you. And now where is he?" he continued. "What have you done with him? He knows much, and the sooner I know it, the better. Are your people bringing him, M. de Berault?"

"No, Monseigneur," I stammered, with dry lips. His very good humour, his benignity, appalled me. I knew how terrible would be the change, how fearful his rage, when I should tell him the truth. And yet that I, Gil de

UNDER THE RED ROBE

Berault, should tremble before any man! I spurred myself, as it were, to the task. "No, Your Eminence," I said, with the courage of despair. "I have not brought him, because I have set him free."

"Because you have--what?" he exclaimed. He leaned forward, his hands on the arm of his chair; and his glittering eyes, growing each instant smaller, seemed to read my soul.

"Because I have let him go," I repeated.

"And why?" he said, in a voice like the rasping of a file.

"Because I took him unfairly," I answered desperately. "Because, Monseigneur, I am a gentleman, and this task should have been given to one who was not. I took him, if you must know," I continued impatiently,-- the fence once crossed, I was growing bolder,--"by dogging a woman's steps, and winning her confidence, and betraying it. And, whatever I have done ill in my life,--of which you were good enough to throw something in my teeth when I was last here,--I have never done that, and I will not!"

"And so you set him free?"

"Yes."

"After you had brought him to Auch?"

"Yes."

"And in point of fact saved him from falling into the hands of the commandant at Auch?"

"Yes," I answered desperately.

"Then what of the trust I placed in you, sirrah?" he rejoined, in a terrible voice; and stooping still farther forward, he probed me with his eyes. "You who prate of trust and confidence, who received your life on parole, and but for your promise to me would have been carrion this month past, answer me that! What of the trust I placed in you?"

"The answer is simple," I said, shrugging my shoulders with a touch of my old self. "I am here to pay the penalty."

"And do you think that I do not know why?" he retorted, striking his one hand on the arm of the chair with a force which startled me. "Because you have heard, Sir, that my power is gone! That I, who was yesterday the King's right hand, am to-day dried up, withered, and paralyzed! Because-- but have a care! Have a care!" he continued not loudly, but in a voice like a dog's snarl. "You, and those others! Have a care I say, or you may find yourselves mistaken yet!"

"As Heaven shall judge me," I answered solemnly, "that is not true. Until I reached Paris last night I knew nothing of this report. I came here with a single mind, to redeem my honour by placing again in Your Eminence's hands that which you gave me on trust."

For a moment he remained in the same attitude, staring at me fixedly. Then his face somewhat relaxed. "Be good enough to ring that bell," he said.

It stood on a table near me. I rang it, and a velvet-footed man in black came in, and gliding up to the Cardinal placed a paper in his hand. The Cardinal looked at it while the man stood with his head obsequiously bent; my heart beat furiously. "Very good," the Cardinal said, after a pause, which seemed to me to be endless. "Let the doors be thrown open."

The man bowed low, and retired behind the screen. I heard a little bell ring, somewhere in the silence, and in a moment the Cardinal stood up. "Follow me!" he said, with a strange flash of his keen eyes.

Astonished, I stood aside while he passed to the screen; then I followed him. Outside the first door, which stood open, we found eight or nine persons,--pages, a monk, the major-domo, and several guards waiting like mutes. These signed to me to precede them, and fell in behind us, and in that order we passed through the first room and the second, where the clerks stood with bent heads to receive us. The last door, the door of the ante-chamber, flew open as we approached; a score of voices cried, "Place! Place for His Eminence!" We passed without pause through two lines of bowing lackeys, and entered--an empty room!

The ushers did not know how to look at one another. The lackeys trembled in their shoes. But the Cardinal walked on, apparently unmoved, until he had passed slowly half the length of the chamber. Then he turned himself about, looking first to one side; and then to another, with a low laugh of derision. "Father," he said, in his thin voice, "what does the psalmist say? 'I am become like a pelican in the wilderness, and like an owl that is in the desert!'"

The monk mumbled assent.

"And later, in the same psalm is it not written, 'They shall perish, but thou shalt endure!'"

"It is so," the father answered. "Amen."

"Doubtless that refers to another life," the Cardinal continued, with his slow, wintry smile. "In the meantime we will go back to our book? and our prayers, and serve God and the King in small things, if not in great. Come, father, this is no longer a place for us. Vanitas vanitatum; omnia vanitas! We will retire."

So, as solemnly as we had come, we marched back through the first and second and third doors, until we stood again in the silence of the Cardinal's chamber; he and I and the velvet-footed man in black. For a while Richelieu seemed to forget me. He stood brooding on the hearth, with his eye's on the embers. Once I heard him laugh; and twice he uttered in a tone of bitter mockery, the words, "Fools! Fools! Fools!"

At last he looked up, saw me, and started. "Ah!" he said. "I had forgotten you. Well, you are fortunate, M. de Berault. Yesterday I had a hundred clients. To-day I have only one, and I cannot afford to hang him. But for your liberty--that is another matter."

I would have said something, but he turned abruptly to the table, and sitting down wrote a few lines on a piece of paper. Then he rang his bell, while I stood waiting and confounded.

The man in black came from behind the screen. "Take that letter and this gentleman to the upper guard-room," His Eminence said sharply. "I can hear no more," he continued wearily, raising his hand to forbid interruption. "The matter is ended, M. de Berault. Be thankful."

And in a moment I was outside the door, my head in a whirl, my heart divided between gratitude and resentment. Along several passages I followed my guide; everywhere finding the same silence, the same monastic stillness. At length, when I had begun to consider whether the Bastile or the Châtelet would be my fate, he stopped at a door, gave me the letter, and, lifting the latch, signed to me to enter.

I went in in amazement, and stopped in confusion. Before me, alone, just risen from a chair, with her face one moment pale, the next red with blushes, stood Mademoiselle de Cocheforêt. I cried out her name.

"M. de Berault!" she said, visibly trembling. "You did not expect to see me?"

"I expected to see no one so little, Mademoiselle," I answered, striving to recover my composure.

"Yet you might have thought that we should not utterly desert you," she replied, with a reproachful humility which went to my heart. "We should have been base indeed, if we had not made some attempt to save you. I thank Heaven that it has so far succeeded that that strange man has promised me your life. You have seen him?" she continued eagerly, and in another tone, while her eyes grew suddenly large with fear.

"Yes, Mademoiselle, I have seen him," I said. "And he has given me my life."

"And?"

"And sent me to imprisonment."

"For how long?" she whispered.

"I do not know," I answered. "I expect, during the King's pleasure."

She shuddered. "I may have done more harm than good," she murmured, looking at me piteously. "But I did it for the best. I told him all, and--yes, perhaps I did harm."

But to hear her accuse herself thus, when she had made this long and lonely journey to save me; when she had forced herself into her enemy's presence, and had, as I was sure she had, abased herself for me, was more than I could bear. "Hush, Mademoiselle, hush!" I said, almost roughly. "You hurt me. You have made me happy: and yet I wish that you were not here, where I fear you have few friends, but back at Cocheforêt. You have done more than I expected, and a hundred times more than I deserved. But I was a ruined man before this happened. I am no more now, but I am still that; and I would not have your name pinned to mine on Paris lips. Therefore, good-bye. God forbid I should say more to you, or let you stay where foul tongues would soon malign you."

She looked at me in a kind of wonder; then with a growing smile, "It is too late," she said gently.

"Too late?" I exclaimed. "How, Mademoiselle?"

"Because--do you remember, M. de Berault, what you told me of your love story, by Agen? That it could have no happy ending? For the same reason I was not ashamed to tell mine to the Cardinal. By this time it is common property."

I looked at her as she stood facing me. Her eyes shone, but they were downcast. Her figure drooped, and yet a smile trembled on her lips. "What did you tell him, Mademoiselle?" I whispered, my breath coming quickly.

"That I loved," she answered boldly, raising her clear eyes to mine. "And therefore that I was not ashamed to beg, even on my knees. Nor ashamed to be with my lover, even in prison."

I fell on my knees, and caught her hand before the last word passed her lips. For the moment I forgot King and Cardinal, prison and the future, all-- all except that this woman, so pure and so beautiful, so far above me in all things, loved me. For the moment, I say. Then I remembered myself. I stood up and thrust her from me, in a sudden revulsion of feeling. "You do not know me," I said. "You do not know me. You do not know what I have done."

"That is what I do know," she answered, looking at me with a wondrous smile.

"Ah, but you do not," I cried. "And besides, there is this--this between us." And I picked up the Cardinal's letter. It had fallen on the floor.

She turned a shade paler. Then she said, "Open it! Open it! It is not sealed, nor closed."

I obeyed mechanically, dreading what I might see. Even when I had it open I looked at the finely scrawled characters with eyes askance. But at last I made it out. It ran thus:--

"The King's pleasure is, that M. de Berault, having mixed himself up with affairs of state, retire forthwith to the manor of Cocheforêt, and confine himself within its limits, until the King's pleasure be further known.

"Richelieu."

On the next day we were married. The same evening we left Paris, and I retraced, in her company, the road which I had twice traversed alone and in heaviness.

A fortnight later we were at Cocheforêt, in the brown woods under the southern mountains; and the great Cardinal, once more triumphant over his enemies, saw, with cold, smiling eyes, the world pass through his chamber. The flood-tide, which then set in, lasted thirteen years; in brief, until his death. For the world had learned its lesson, and was not to be deceived a second time. To this hour they call that day, which saw me stand for all his friends, "The day of Dupes."

THE END

CPSIA information can be obtained
at www.ICGtesting.com
Printed in the USA
LVHW081546070319
609854LV00033B/724/P